Lacrimosa

Song of the Sphere

A. W. Brame

Book Cover by A. W. Brame
Edits done by Heather W.

Paperback edition published 2025
ISBN: 979-8-218-58921-9

To my wife, Abby.
You are the love of my life and my best friend.
I love you to the moon and back!

To Lukas and Katie,
Friends who put up with my ridiculousness, without ever demanding compensation.
You guys are one in a million!

To my mother,
You gave me life and taught me the joys of reading.
I'm probably not, "where I'm supposed to be, when I'm supposed to be."

To Herman Melville, H.G. Wells, J.R.R. Tolkien, and C.S. Lewis.
You taught me to go on adventures, dream wildly and vividly, and aim for the stars.
The enrichment you have added to my life knows no bounds.

To Christ,
You saved me in a thousand ways.
Here I am, send me.

One

Arrival

1

The heat of the 92-degree day was beating down on Olivia Jane fiercely as she tried to reposition herself, the injury in her leg protesting painfully at the attempt. Laying in the front yard and tending to the tree that she had planted for her father had proven to be a much more challenging job than she had anticipated. She was, however, bound and determined to finish the task, regardless of what interjections her leg posed. And despite the summer's heat.

Olivia was tired of sitting in the house with nothing to do. Her friends from college had visited her from time to time, but it was now few and far between as they were wrapped up in their studies, schedules, and attending parties as college freshmen at the University of Wisconsin – La Crosse, where she should be too. Where she should still be. She had been a college freshman, until a man who had been driving under the influence, struck her with his vehicle while she was crossing the intersection on East Avenue North after spending a warm afternoon in Myrick Park. The collision had thrown her several feet, rendering her unconscious. It wasn't until later, waking up in Gundersen Lutheran Hospital that she discovered her right femur had been broken and displaced at the lower end, and her foot had a few broken metatarsals. This left her needing two surgeries and left her out of class for two semesters. She was, however, hopeful to return in the upcoming semester.

She had spent a few months in the hospital, then longer in physical therapy. Not to mention the two surgeries. The doctor had given her an estimated recovery time of a year. And that date was coming up. She had come a long way now, but the leg brace was still required.

As was medication for pain management. Olivia despised every moment of it. She frequently moved out to the living room of the house for a much-needed change of scenery from her bedroom. To make matters even worse, she had been mostly alone during this time.

It had been over two years now since the cancer had taken her father, and the house still haunted her with the silence his absence created. The house, as quiet as it had become, was the final gift her father had given her and her brother. He worked hard to pay off the modest three-bedroom home. Olivia didn't know it at the time, but he had worked towards this goal even after he became aware of the diagnosis.

When he was asked why he did this he simply replied, "I wanted to leave something behind for you, kids." He was only on hospice for two weeks after Olivia found out about the cancer. Leaving her and her older brother, Adam, alone in the house.

Adam had withdrawn into an angry ball of isolation years ago when their mom left. Graduating high school four years before Olivia. Although he still lived in the house, work and friends were where most of his time was spent. On the rare occasions that he was home, he would isolate in his room with the door closed and the music he was listening to or the game he was playing acting as a second wall to keep the world out. "It's just the way he is processing your mom leaving," her father would say. Olivia regretted never asking her father how he handled Mom leaving. It happened when she was younger, and she was too distracted with her own life, as many kids in junior high school are, at that time.

Their mother met another man, and left to live with him in Arizona. She started another family with him there. A family that Olivia has only seen in social media photos. In the time since her mother left, Olivia had only seen her a handful of times. It used to be once a year. But it had been three years now since she had seen her face. Even when her father died. Adam had refused to see her at all.

Weirdly, the accident that Oliva had faced had brought her and Adam closer than they had been in years. He had been there for her in the hospital, getting into a shouting match with a nurse once over Oliva being left in an uncomfortable position for too long.

With her at home, he would check in on her through texts and the occasional phone call to see if she needed anything. He was very good at keeping the refrigerator stocked, which Olivia greatly appreciated.

The contact between them was limited now. But, if she had a need, he would get it for her. He did go to Menards and get her the bag of mulch that she was currently using around the tree in the front yard. "Are you going to be able to handle that with your leg?" he asked skeptically when he brought it into the garage.

"Of course," she replied, though the doubt was indeed in her mind. This morning, she went out to the garage and found the bag cut open and a five-gallon bucket placed next to it. Seems Adam doubted. In defiance, Olivia positioned her weight onto her good leg and attempted to lift the large bag of mulch, only to quickly find that this was not going to work. She silently resigned to take the small garden trowel and fill the bucket he had left for her. "You win, Adam," she muttered under her breath.

Walking with one crutch under her right arm to support her leg, and carrying the bucket in her left arm had been significantly harder than she was willing to admit, but she was able to limp out to the tree in the front yard. The first trip was hard, the second trip was even more difficult, now, laying on the soft grass next to the small tree after her third trip, Olivia was seriously considering putting any further trips off for later in the day. Her leg was aching and her pain management medication far away in the house – a fact Olivia was currently kicking herself over.

The small tree that Olivia had planted was relatively well covered now at its base with the mulch, she still wanted to encircle the space with some kind of stone or something else decorative. She had planted this tree sometime after her father had died, and though he already had a grave and headstone, she still came to the tree and thought of her father as one might when visiting a gravestone. It was planted close to the road in the front yard of their home. An odd place to be sure, but for Olivia, the placement was irrelevant. Her father had used his final time here to make sure her brother and her would have a home, she wanted to leave a memorial of sorts for him.

Olivia removed the hair tie that she had around her wrist and threw her long, dark brown, wavy hair into a quick, messy bun. Normally, she wore her hair down to cover her ears, which she considered large and unattractive. But, she wanted her hair off her neck to allow the air to cool her, in the sweltering heat.

The sound of shouting drew her attention from her struggle, across the road to the small blue house that sat opposite hers. The front window of the house was open and the voices from within could be heard. Olivia didn't need to see the people to know who they were and what was happening. The husband was drunk, and he was yelling at his wife. This had been happening for years, and little had changed.

One night, the wife, a small whisper of a woman named Tiffany, knocked on the door. Olivia's father answered the door to find Tiffany with a bruised face and holding her daughter, Nina, in her arms.

Olivia's father had sent her to her room. Later, when she asked her father about it, he simply said. "Our neighbors just needed a safe place for a little bit." Adam, ever the quick-to-respond type, had asked if the cops had been called. Her father just shook his head sadly. In the years since, Olivia had heard and seen much evidence of the terror that Rick, the husband and father, reigned on his family. She often worried about little Nina, and the effects of daily trauma she experienced.

The arguing abruptly stopped, and Olivia sat for a few moments, listening. She had long wanted to call the police, but the truth was that even if the police were called, there was little that could be done. After all, if Tiffany wouldn't report what was happening, what could they do?

She often found herself saddened by it all. Saddened by her brother for being cold, isolated, and angry all the time. Saddened by her mother for choosing the affair and "following her heart" over her own family. Saddened by the woman across the street for not standing up to her drunk husband, and not protecting her child. Saddened by Rick's choice of booze over his family's wellness. Saddened because her first year in college had been away from her by some man driving drunk at ten in the morning. She tilted her head up, looking to the sky for some kind of answer, but saw none.

2

It moved slowly through the inky back cold void, as it had for thousands of years, wandering, and searching for something. Something like it. Yet, for eons and eons, all it found was cold, empty dead space. Many of the celestial sights it had seen were beautiful. Planets with fascinating landscapes dancing around burning stars. Massive blooms of gas suspended in the void in spectacular colors that stretched far and wide. Magnificent evidence of He who created it. But, still, no sign of Him, or anything else alive and aware, like it was. It knew He would return one day.

For now, it was alone.

It spotted another warm and inviting star, floating in the void. Moving towards it, it took note of the curious objects around. A gorgeous yellow planet, ringed with beauty, past it, another body, red with rust. Then, ahead. Closer to the warmth of the star, it felt a hum unlike any it had heard before. Yet this place was familiar to it, its memory fogged by thousands of years. Closer and closer it drew, the hum becoming more intricate and more vibrant. With boundless excitement, it moved toward the small blue planet.

It was no longer alone.

Could this be it? Could this be the world He created? The creator had said when the time was right, this would happen. That it would find its way back to where it had all begun. And it had.

The small blue planet had changed dramatically since it was here last. Small objects floated around it, and though they weren't alive, they hummed with some strange electrical fever, speaking to the planet in a strange, rapid and bizarre pattern. The humans were still there, on the face of the planet. They moved and gathered and constructed large areas where they lived together. But the closer it looked, the more saddened and confused it became.

The verdant green that made this world so unique had been replaced by the humans with cold and ugly stone, metal, and barren dirt. But, why? Looking closer, it could see that there were other beings, formless, and were unnoticed by the humans, who created things that destroyed the life around them. It knew these beings; these were the ones who were meant to guide them. Why had they not, what had happened?

To discover what had gone wrong, it peered deep into the humans. It found the living essence, much like its own, inside of them, the thing they called the soul. The deeper it looked inside of this, the more horrified it became. There were levels of greed, anger, and cruelty that it couldn't ever have conceived of or imagined. This ugliness of the humans oozed out of their souls and into the way they treated each other. At their center was the darkness. The darkness that had been fought so long ago. It ruled them now. The darkness had survived, and had become the ruler of this world.

The planet was still covered with life, but it also crawled with death. The cursed one sat at the center of all of it.

It decided that it would no longer wonder. It would remain here. Waiting for the Creator to return. In the meantime, there was work to do here.

3

Lying in her bed, Olivia stared intently and wide-eyed at the screen of her phone. Every news media station, every social media platform, every voice everywhere was talking about the strange object that had appeared just beyond the moon's orbit. Pictures and videos of it were everywhere. There wasn't a single news station, social media company, celebrity, or influencer that was not obsessing over the thing that had appeared in the sky.

When the information and images of the object first started to come out, they were all grainy. It was nearly impossible to make out what it looked like other than a white, out-of-focus snowball against a black backdrop. Many were denying it to be real. For a few hours, that was all the information that was coming out: scientists claiming that an object had appeared, and news outlets releasing the blurry images. Debates and conversations raged, but no definitive reports were made. Meanwhile, social media exploded with end-of-the-world predictions.

Then, the object did something, something that no one on the planet had stopped talking about for the last few hours. It moved. "The Sphere," as they were now calling it, suddenly moved into an orbit directly above Earth. Though, in truth, no one could say for sure that it did move. Rather it simply appeared in its new location. Some reported that it "moved suddenly," and others said that it "jumped" – instantly moving to the new location. Regardless of how people described the method with which it moved, everyone agreed on something: it had changed its course, somehow.

Everyone was now debating exactly what this meant. Most of the voices Olivia heard through her phone seemed to believe that what they were looking at was a massive spacecraft of some kind, and that aliens from another world were piloting it. Phrases like "We are not alone," and "First Contact" filled the screen of Olivia's phone, and the world was abuzz with the prospect of aliens.

A group of people assembled in the desert of California and made massive signs, lit bonfires, and gathered to welcome them. The eclectic group of people called themselves "The Welcome Party." People with crystals and hippie clothing were explaining to the news, and on their social media pages that the aliens had come to spiritually enlighten everyone, and that everyone should get rid of what they referred to as "bad vibrations."

"It will be a new era of awareness and oneness with the universe," a woman explained, who had what appeared to be a crystal tied in a braid around her forehead. Behind her, a group of people sat in a circle with their faces pointed up to the sky, while others danced erratically around a fire.

Another swipe on Olivia's phone brought her to a livestream of a politician with a blue tie and an expensive suit, standing at a podium in front of the press explaining that the reason the aliens had arrived was that they recognized and were inspired to make contact because of the social reform that his party and his office had been implementing. "I believe these visitors are prepared to contact us because of the social and economic reforms within our government, brought about by the tireless efforts of our party."

Olivia swiped again, scoffing at the man. This brought her to the page of a social media influencer who was modeling some clothing for the viewer. "It's going to be so important to let them know that you are culturally diverse because then they will want to be your friend. So, that's why I assembled this outfit today! It has, like, lots of different culture and tradition stuff, so they can see how aware of my planet I am." Olivia rolled her eyes, and closed the window.

She scrolled down to a single image of the Sphere. The image was taken after it had moved closer to Earth and had been photographed by an observatory. It was dark gray, with black lines crisscrossing its surface, and these lines seemed to have no discernable pattern. At some of the line's intersections were odd pale gray circles of varying sizes. These were not craters as they did not indent into the object but were simply unknown markings on its smooth surface. A news commentator had compared them to eyes and wondered if they were monitoring stations for the object.

She had seen this picture a thousand times already and it didn't show anything new, however, the person who posted the photo had added the text: "Nothing will ever be the same," under it.

Olivia closed the social media app and opened her texting app. She scrolled down to the message she had sent to Adam earlier, asking where he was and if he had seen what was happening. Seeing that he still hadn't replied, she felt a well of frustration bubble up. She shot off another text, something that she tried not to do normally when he didn't reply, but this was not a normal situation. "Where are you? Seriously, Adam, please answer."

She couldn't help but feel completely helpless. Not only because of the object in the sky, and the mass hysteria it was causing across the planet, but she felt helpless because she was indeed helpless. Lying in bed, with her leg in the brace, too tired to do much, and alone in the house. She felt abandoned by her brother, which wasn't exactly something new, but this was different. She was scared and alone. She needed someone. She considered texting her mother but decided against it. She couldn't handle being ignored by her too. Not now.

Olivia couldn't help but imagine horrible scenarios of alien intruders coming into her home. Where she would be powerless to defend herself. She pictured terrifying green aliens, with large unfeeling black eyes, looking down on her while she lay helplessly in bed. Would they kill her? Shoot her with some alien ray gun? Or would they carry her away and take her to some horrible room Where they would carry out terrifying experiments?

The ding from her phone pulled out of her paranoid dreaming. It was Adam. "Sorry Liv, out with work friends. End of the world party! Don't wait up for me. This is crazy!" For a moment, Olivia considered throwing the phone across the room but decided against it considering that she would have to hobble over to get it. Instead, she slammed it down on the bed, took a moment to control her breathing, then calmly picked it back up.

"I'm just glad you are ok. Come home when you can, I don't want to be alone," she replied. She knew that if she were too pushy, he may ignore it completely. It aggravated her that she needed to tip-toe like this with him, but he was the only family that she had left.

Couldn't he have at least thought about her before going out?

Staring up at the dark ceiling, Oliva was trying to fight back tears of isolation, fear, and hopelessness. She did well for a while, but she soon felt overwhelmed with a deep need. She thought of how much she wanted to hear her father's voice reassuring her that it was going to be ok and that she wasn't alone. She thought about how his soft and kind smile, and his calm demeanor could put her at ease, even in the most stressful of solutions. She thought of how much she missed him, and how badly she needed him now. She couldn't put up the fight any longer and began to cry. The sounds of her crying fell on the unreactive walls and furniture of the empty house.

Far above, The Sphere heard.

4

The next morning came quickly for Olivia. It was just before six in the morning and the first trace of morning light was beginning to show itself as a dull blue hue through her window. Olivia began to roll over to go back to sleep, but the reality of yesterday's arrival jarred her mind wide awake. Firstly, green malevolent aliens did not abduct her in the night, as she had been fearful of. Secondly, it was daytime now. Perhaps she could go outside and see it for herself.

She slowly and clumsily got out of bed, her leg screaming in painful protest – as it did most mornings. She grabbed her large, blue robe and hobbled out of the bedroom and into the hallway. The light was dim, but she could see that the door to Adam's room was closed, which probably meant that he was home and inside. As she continued to the living room, she spotted his truck in the driveway. It was a sure sign that he was home. Olivia was desperately tempted to barge into his room and scold him for leaving her alone. She decided against it, however, knowing she would only be met with irritation, both from him, and for him. Instead, she decided to continue to the front yard and see if she could spot the object for herself. She grabbed her crutch, and she stepped outside.

Olivia was expecting to have a difficult time spotting the Sphere, thinking it would be like looking for a specific star or trying to find a constellation at night. In contrast, the Sphere was not hard to see. It seemed to be hanging in the sky, hovering directly above her. As she staired at it, she was filled with a sense of impending doom. It seemed so close that it could fall on her at any moment.

It hovered inside the atmosphere. The pictures from the night before portrayed the Sphere differently: here, it seemed more light grey, and the bizarre lines and circles on it were easier to see than the social media pictures had been. Olivia was certain that she had seen planes in the area flying at relatively the same altitude as the mysterious object. The scene reminded her of an old game her brother played when he was younger, about a little cartoon boy who had three days to stop the moon from crashing into the earth. The moon, in this game, had a face with a terrified expression and would get larger in the sky as the days passed.

Olivia held up her hand at arm's length, with her fingers in a fist and her thumb up. She used her thumb as a sort of measurement against the Sphere. It's diameter was about the same length as from the tip of her thumb to where her thumb disappears into her palm. Taking up more real estate in the sky then the moon or the sun did.

Still, it loomed in the sky, and looking up at it and feeling its weight hovering in the air gave her a sense of vertigo.

She looked away and found her attention drawn to her neighbors sitting in their front yard. They had pulled out lawn chairs and a small foldable camping table, they were looking at their phones which were playing loudly. The wife's phone was playing a newscast and the host was arguing angrily with someone on their show. "You don't know a damn thing, I don't care how many books you have written, how dare you come on here and act like you speak with some authority. You don't know any more about the aliens than I do," he shouted. The other person was trying to interrupt but with no success.

Balancing on her good leg, Olivia pulled her phone out of the robe's pocket and turned it on. A short time of scrolling showed her what she had already discovered through her observations. During the night, the Sphere had moved into the earth's atmosphere and had begun hovering above her town of La Crosse, Wisconsin. Something that she didn't know, however, was that several aircraft of different types had attempted to get close to it but had all failed. A mysterious total system failure had occurred for any aircraft that flew within 25 miles of the sphere. There were posts about a few helicopters from the military that had gone down attempting to push through to the Sphere.

The La Crosse Regional Airport had been shut down and was currently serving as a base of operations for the military. A few of the news channels and pages Oliva was looking at showed images of military personnel brandishing weapons and riding in Humvees and armored vehicles at the airport. The reporter for the local news was reporting that the military was refusing to comment, but she did say that members of the military's scientific community were present on sight.

The newscaster then changed topics, and began discussing the planned evacuation of La Crosse. The order was expected to have been made last night, but the governor had delayed it for now. Many speculated as to why the delay had been called, but nothing definitive was reported.

Continuing to scroll, Olivia saw that mass hysteria had taken over in many places. Rioting and protests were happening in Chicago and New York. A large group of people in California had laid down in the street of Los Angeles and poisoned themselves, the images of bodies covered in sheets were posted with the headline: "Did the Aliens Make Them Do It?". In a foreign country that Olivia did not recognize, some rebels had taken over the capital and were publicly executing the government officials that they had captured. And, on every news station, there were people debating, yelling at one another, playing clips of the various world leaders telling everyone to remain calm, only for people to accuse them of keeping the truth from everyone. It was beyond overwhelming, and Olivia felt herself becoming dizzy and sick to her stomach with anxiety.

She looked up at the Sphere. If there were aliens or something of the sort inside of it, what must they be thinking now, watching all of this unfold? Olivia couldn't help but think that they, or it, could only be horrified by what was happening down here. Not just since the Sphere arrived, but also the scope of human history. Wars, genocide, the Holocaust, the bombings of Hiroshima and Nagasaki, the pollution of our planet, the giant island of plastic that was floating in the Pacific Ocean, and the countless other atrocities that have been and are accruing all over the globe.

We are an awful species, Olivia thought to herself. Even on an individual scale, her own mother had abandoned her. If that wasn't enough evidence of how broken we humans were, Olivia didn't know what was.

"I hope you are here to fix us," Olivia said in a low voice to the Sphere. The sound of the arguing newscaster continued to play from her neighbor's phone. "We need it," she concluded.

A few moments after these words left Olivia's lips, a deep thud came from the Sphere, like an explosion deep underwater, only this was far up in the sky. The sound was followed a moment later by a sensation like an invisible wave passing over Olivia. She staggered a step, more out of surprise than any physical effect the wave had. The wave did seem to have a physical effect on some things though, the plants and trees swayed slightly at its effect. As if a small gust of wind had brushed them. That was not the most dramatic impact the wave had, however. All the electricity and power everywhere seemed to go off all at once. The homes that had their lights on all went dark, a car that was heading down the street went quiet and slowly drifted to a stop on the road, the loud cell phones of the neighbors that had previously been blasting now fell silent, their owners looking around urgently and trying to power them back on. Olivia checked her phone, it did not turn on either. In the distance, the ever-constant hum of the highway suddenly fell silent, this was then suddenly shattered by the sound of cars crashing, first one, then two, then a quick cascading sound that then fell silent itself. In the distance, Olivia could hear voices starting to pick up. Even her neighbors, who had previously only been giving attention to the screens in their hands, were now urgently chatting with one another. Olivia's gaze returned to the Sphere, it hung silently in the sky, seeming to look down on her with the strange circle shapes on its face.

A very real feeling of dread came over Olivia.

A few hours had passed, since the Sphere had robbed everyone of their electricity. Nearly everyone in the neighborhood was now standing outside and urgently discussing this situation. It surprised Olivia when she realized how many people she did not know. After all, she had lived in this neighborhood most of her life, and since the accident, had been almost exclusively at home. Yet, she had never laid eyes on many of the people she now was speaking with. Olivia marveled at the fact that she had spent so much of her life so close to these people yet didn't know any of them. Many of these strangers were still holding their phones in their hands and would occasionally try to power them back on.

As different as they all were, they all did have something in common. Everyone was without power. The water, however, was still flowing through everyone's faucets. Many of the people were debating about how this was possible. Answers ranged from it not being on the electrical grid, to the area having good water towers. Even with good water towers, however, eventually, the water in the faucets would run out if power wasn't restored to run the pumps that filled the towers.

One man, a guy, whom Olivia discovered to be named Greg, had an opinion on everything. He spoke as if his opinions were well-known facts, and was willing to argue with anyone who possessed a contrary opinion.

"I'm just saying that what is happening is obvious to anyone with half a brain," he loudly spoke over the others. "What just happened was what is called an EMP attack," with the letters E-M-P slowed down and accentuated. "That means, an Electromagnetic Pulse. It knocks out all electronics in its blast radius. That's why nothing is working. So, it's obvious that the next thing the aliens are going to do is to send in a ground invasion now that we can't communicate and coordinate an effective defense."

"Well, I don't know about all that," a woman named Sue replied, condescension dripping from her voice. Sue had been the neighbor who was outside on her phone earlier, and though she had indeed been involved with the discussions being had, she hardly ever had anything constructive to say. Rather, her contribution was usually hyper-criticism of all other ideas. "If there were some kind of invasion happening, the news would have warned us about it. I've been watching the news all night;

the experts haven't mentioned a peep about some kind of ESP attack." The voices of the group rose to this, some in agreement and some in disagreement. "This is America, the news doesn't lie to us here."

"It's called an EMP, not ESP," Greg retorted. "If they are not planning to attack, then why else would they knock out our power?"

"Well, I don't know, but assuming the worst about our visitors won't help us. We must be inclusive when they come. Nothing has happened yet, so they are obviously peaceful." The crowd began arguing once again over this, voices clashing into an incoherent cacophony of noise. Sue tried to get the crowd to vote for who they thought was correct, so that they could then decide on what to do next. She said that if the aliens did show up, it should be her who does the talking. "We need someone with an open mind," she boldly announced. Olivia decided that she had had enough of this conversation, and that the growing pain in her leg was also done with it. She resolved to head towards the house to see if Adam had woken up yet.

She began to hobble her way through the group in the direction of her home. The people did little to help. They were all too busy arguing with one another to even notice that she was struggling on her crutch to get through them. Olivia noticed a familiar face standing off to the side of the group. It was Tiffany, who now seemed to be in her thirties, and her daughter Nina. Tiffany wasn't saying anything, just listening to the group argue with each other. Her face seemed desperate though, urgently listening for an answer to what was happening. Nina stood at her mother's side, she was clutching her mom's arm, watching as well.

Olivia felt the need to walk over and comfort them, tell them that no one knew for sure what was happening, and that it was ok to be scared. She paused for a moment and realized that the pain in her leg would not allow this trip, urging her to go back inside instead. She locked eyes with Tiffany whose worry and fear were plainly written on her face. Olivia gave a soft smile, one that she hoped would communicate the things she wanted to say. Tiffany smiled back but her eyes still had the same longing for answers or help.

Olivia decided to push through the pain. She hobbled over on her crutch to Tiffany and her daughter, who now seemed to be elementary school age. Olivia had been blessed with an amazing father, and her heart broke for the little girl who was not as fortunate.

Olivia hadn't been exactly sure of what she was going to say. *Hi there, crazy alien invasion we are having, Hu?* No, that was terrible. As she passed the arguing group, she decided that the best thing to do right now was to be human. To see how she was doing, rather than speculate like the rest into insanity.

"How are you holding up," she asked when she reached the woman.

Tiffany breathed a sigh of relief. "Freaked out, you?"

"Very freaked out." Olivia replied.

They continued speaking to one another for a short time. Olivia focused on seeing how Tiffany and her daughter were doing rather than speculating about the Sphere. As to be expected, they were scared and didn't know anything. Olivia shared that she felt the same way. Olivia did ask about the husband, Rick. "Oh, he's still asleep," Tiffany answered, then quickly changed the subject, asking Olivia about the tree in the yard. Olivia dropped the matter of the husband, suspecting that he was simply sleeping off the alcohol.

5

Eventually, hunger drove many, including Olivia, back into their homes. With the power still out, the lack of electrical lights made the homes like dark caves. All the shades on the windows had to be opened to make vision possible. Olivia took a moment to try a flashlight that was in a drawer in the kitchen, it too yielded no light. It seemed that all electronics, regardless of how small, were inoperable. She went to the refrigerator and discovered food silently sitting in the dark. Two thoughts dawned on Olivia, the first was how strange it was to open a refrigerator and find food sitting silently in the dark. Secondly, and more troublingly, she realized that the food would spoil quickly with no refrigeration being applied to it. It was essentially a glorified cooler at this moment. Still, she threw together a sandwich and ate. It was at this moment that she considered the comment about water eventually running out if the power wasn't restored. So, she found all the bottles she could and her collection of thermoses and began filling them in the kitchen sink. She even finished a bottle of orange juice and set it on the counter to be filled with water later. She wouldn't be able to cool them, but she would have water.

She had just finished filling up the second thermos with water when she heard the door to Adam's room open, and Adam shuffle to the bathroom. She heard him try the light switch a few times, then shut the door. A few moments later he flushed the toilet and appeared in the kitchen. "Morning Liv," he said. "Any idea what's going on with the power?" Olivia explained to him all that she had seen. She described the wave that came out of the Sphere, how the power died, and even the theories of Greg the neighbor. Adam shook his head, "Hope he's wrong about that." Olivia agreed and then explained why she was filling thermoses with water. "Smart," Adam replied in approval, as he too assembled a sandwich. He paused for a moment, "Is dad's shotgun still in the basement? You know, just in case."

"Yes," Olivia replied. She had been considering the Mossberg 500 that Dad had left in the basement. She hoped dearly that she wouldn't need to use it in some interstellar conflict of survival against an alien invader. Not to mention her current physical limitations. If something happened, if the situation came to a question of survival, Olivia was sure that she wouldn't be able to defend herself. "Adam, can you please stay? At least until we know what this situation is," she asked Adam, cautiously.

Adam thought for a second, chewing the sandwich he had made. "Sure," he casually replied. Olivia could have walked over and hugged him for this. "We were going to have another end-of-the-world night tonight, but I can chill here instead."

"Thank you, Adam," Olivia said emphatically. "I didn't want to spend another night by myself with all this happening."

Adam paused for a second. "So, what has the cow said about this whole thing," he asked. The tone of mockery was always in his voice whenever he asked about their mother, he also had taken to addressing her as "the cow." Olivia had long decided that as much as Adam pretended that he didn't care about Mom, she was still important to him. If he truly didn't care, he wouldn't hate her so much. But, this was hardly a fact that Olivia was about to point out now. No, as much as her brother liked to convey an attitude of irreverence with many things, he was still sensitive and reactive. His indifferent demeanor was merely a wall, behind which rested hurt and anger. She wasn't about to try and tear down that wall. Not now. If she were critical of him, he would simply leave, and she would be alone. Deep down, she resented him for this. She felt trapped by this scenario of her needing not to offend him and let him do whatever it was that he wanted, so he would not abandon her. In truth, she was afraid Adam was too much like their mother.

"Actually," Olivia said with reluctance. "Mom hasn't messaged me."

"Classic," Adam responded bitterly.

Olivia turned and began filling another thermos with water, deciding to occupy herself with a task rather than join Adam in hating their mother. She was already hurt by her mother's lack of concern.

"So," Adam chimed. "What do you think the big thing in the sky is?"

"I don't know, everyone is saying it's aliens," she replied. "If it is, I still don't understand why they haven't tried to contact us."

Adam paused for a moment before replying. "I think it's because they have plans for the world, and they aren't too concerned with what our opinion about those plans are."

Adam finished his food and then returned to his room to change his clothes. He wanted to go outside and see the Sphere also but clearly stated that he was not interested in talking to the neighbors. Deciding, instead, to go into the backyard. Olivia continued to fill the thermoses. She finished filling the four thermoses that she had and began to fill the emptied orange juice jug when she became aware of some kind of commotion happening outside. She finished filling the jug, set it on the counter next to the others, and turned off the faucet so that she could clearly hear what was happening.

Raised voices of both men and women could be heard arguing. Olivia strained to hear what was being said in the mix, remaining still for a few moments. A loud cry of "Rick, please stop," immediately sent Olivia rushing out to help. It was Tiffany's voice, and the Rick she was speaking of was undoubtedly her husband. Olivia was in such a hurry to help, she neglected to grab her crutch, unintentionally leaving it leaning against the counter by the sink.

Once outside, she found Rick holding the daughter's arm roughly and yelling at her in slurred speech. "Tell me, tell me now! What did your idiot mother do to the lights!" The group of neighbors had seemingly gathered again outside. Greg, the know-it-all, and Sue, the self-appointed ambassador for humanity, were both shocked and silently watching, neither intervening in the situation.

Tiffany was on her knees, pleading with her husband. "Please stop! Everyone's power is out! I didn't do anything, I swear!"

Greg piped up, "It was the aliens," his voice was significantly lacking the confidence it had before.

"You think I'm stupid," Rick snapped back, then turned to his wife. "Your new boyfriend is an idiot, going on about aliens!" Many in the crowd implored him to look up, but he refused. "You all think I'm some kind of idiot?" Still refusing to look up at the Sphere dangling directly above his head.

The daughter took advantage of this situation and stepped into her father, then pushed him off balance. His grip remained strong on her arm, and he fell still clutching her tiny arm. She let out a squeal of pain. He used her to stand back up, then shoved her down to the ground violently, the small crowd now was shouting incoherently. Rick shouted curses wildly, then locked eyes with his wife and made a lunge for her, his teeth bare in a rage-filled snarl.

Seemingly out of nowhere, Adam came from the crowd, a lead pipe in his hands, and he drove it into the stomach of Rick like a spear, who promptly doubled over and fell onto his side. Greg suddenly got brave once again, and in a confident voice said, "just stay down."

Rick got back up awkwardly, his fists balled, glaring hatefully at his wife and daughter. "I'm going to kill you for that!"

Up above, the low distant boom sounded again. Everyone froze and looked up. Even Rick. Greg exclaimed, "it's starting!" Whatever, "it" was Olivia didn't know, and she was sure he didn't either.

A long, deep, and resonating sound came from the Sphere, like a massive unseen trumpet bellowing out. It started low then steadily grew more powerful. As its bizarre note rose, Rick covered his ears and cursed something unintelligible, then slurred, "Get out! Get out of my head." The first bellow faded. Everything was silent. A silence like Olivia had never heard before. As if time, space, and matter were all holding their breath in anxious anticipation.

The bellowing came again, this time it was deafening. The ground shook with its resonance and Olivia could feel it moving through her body in numbing vibrations. Most people fell to the ground, including Olivia. Adam did not, he instead grabbed Olivia and hoisted her up, half carrying, half dragging her to the house. Behind her, Olivia could hear the neighbors scream and saw a few of them flee into their own homes. Rick remained where he was on the lawn. He was clawing at his face, leaving crimson tear marks in his flesh. Laughing hysterically.

The bellowing sounded again and again, at different lengths and intervals. Every time it sounded, waves of distortion and violent tremors would rock the surroundings. Trees were swaying back and forth, cars in the driveway heaved and rocked, and houses groaned and shifted with some of their glass windows shattering. Adam opened the front door, now carrying Olivia completely. He dragged her down the hall and to the basement door. "Get in, get in," he shouted. Without thinking, she stepped into the doorway and heard the door slam behind her, only slightly aware that Adam had not followed her into the stairwell. Dizzy and disoriented, and without her crutch, she went down the stairs into the basement. The bellowing continued, the sound was slightly muffled, but it still shook the ground and caused a feeling like rippling water to pass over Olivia.

She continued down into the unfinished basement, but her leg brace was clumsy and she fell hard against the cinderblock wall, completely unable to feel the pain of the impact over the waves and bellowing. From down here, with the bellowing muffled slightly by her earth and concrete surroundings, Olivia vaguely noticed that the bellowing seemed to have a sort of "flow" to it, like a song being sung in some language that she didn't understand. The melody of the bellowing repeated, tones and pitches became apparent, and its rhythm and pattern remained consistent, shaking the world with its ferocity and power. The disorientation and dizziness soon overtook her, and Olivia slumped down and slipped into unconsciousness.

6

Olivia woke, unsure of how much time had passed. The bellowing continued outside but seemed to shake the ground less, and the strange feelings of distortion and dizziness seemed to also have lessened. Now, however, Olivia could hear distant rumblings that seemed to sound out from the earth around her. She could feel and hear the tremors and shifting of the earth, as if far-off massive creatures of some kind were adjusting and moving to new places and pulling the earth around with them. The unfinished basement shook at times with this, dirt and dust would fall from the bare ceiling rafters as the rumbling tremors sounded. The bellowing still softly continued above.

No longer feeling the disorienting effects of the bellowing, Olivia began to move, getting into a position so that she could stand without causing her leg too much pain. About halfway through this maneuver, Olivia realized the pain that normally accompanied such a task was not present. She flexed her knee and rotated her leg around tentatively and found there was no pain. She felt that she could move it rather freely. She removed her brace and stood up, putting her weight on the leg, and let out a surprised gasp that there was no pain at all.

A rumbling nearby sounded, and the ground shook again. Above Olivia, the house groaned with it, causing her to crouch down and duck in fear of a collapse. It didn't happen, nor did the pain come back to her leg, despite this rapid physical exertion. It was at this moment that she realized that Adam was not present. "Adam,"

Olivia called out. There was no reply. She moved over to the stairwell and shouted out for him again. Still, there was no reply. There was no sound of any kind. The bellowing song that the Sphere had been playing was no longer filling the air, shaking the earth with its intensity, or casting its rippling waves.

Cautiously, Olivia opened the door leading out of the basement, the house was still dark, and extensive damage had been done. Large cracks had formed across the walls, a portion of the living room ceiling had collapsed down, and most of the windows that Olivia could see were broken, and the sun shined brightly. Olivia again shouted Adam's name, to which there was, again, no reply. She then went to the front door and opened it.

As the door swung open, Olivia's eyes took in a completely different world. The sun was shining brightly and warmly, warmer than it had been before, and the light showed upon a new and lush landscape. The grass was long and tall with wildflowers and plant life filling the once short and green grass with vibrant color and variety. The road had been overgrown and somewhat broken apart with grass, weeds, and even small trees growing through it. The once sparse trees that had dotted the residential street had nearly doubled in size, and there seemed to be more of them. They reached proudly into the sky, towering over the homes of the neighborhood. The homes were now mostly overgrown with vegetation, and many appeared to have collapsed. Olivia looked back at her own home to discover that it too was covered in vegetation.

However, the change that grabbed Olivia's attention the most rested in what had once been her front yard. There, stood the tree Olivia had been tending to only yesterday. It was massive. Its trunk had almost filled the yard now and went through the road and occupied part of the neighbor's yard, a diameter of at least forty feet. The tree towered high into the sky, far above anything else around it, and birds flew calmly around its massive structure. Olivia felt as though she were gazing up at a skyscraper standing mightily in the center of a city, and not the modest neighborhood of Wedgewood Terrace, La Crosse. Through the branches of the massive tree, which had been only a tiny Oak tree, barely taller than Olivia herself just a few hours ago, the Sphere seemed to peer back at her.

Olivia took all of this in for several moments, she could hardly believe her eyes. As terrifying as the whole situation was, she couldn't help but be completely enamored with the beauty of this new world. She didn't understand why, or how, this thing in the sky had done this. But she felt, deep down in the depths of her soul, that it was good. She felt deep in her spirit that something that had previously been broken in the world was somehow mended, just as the brokenness in her leg had been. She also felt something else deep in her soul. A truth that she had not known before, but that she knew to be true now. The Sphere was alive. It wasn't a ship that was filled with little green aliens. No, it was its own entity somehow. Alive and aware, looking down at her with some intention and purpose that she could perhaps not comprehend. Olivia had no idea how she knew this information, rather that she simply just did. The way that you feel sunlight on your face and recognize what it is without seeing it for yourself.

Olivia looked around for anyone else. She saw no one, not even Rick who had been left in the front yard of his home. She shuddered as she remembered the things that he had said when the Sphere began singing.

Something about, "get out of my head." What did that mean? Whatever the Sphere did, it affected him very differently than it affected her. She decided that she needed to be cautious. After all, who knew what this new world harbored? It all seemed beautiful and filled with the natural beauty of nature. But nature was also violent, and very dangerous. True, she could sense that something had been corrected in this world. But that doesn't necessarily mean that everything is safe now.

She called out for Adam, but there was, again, no reply. She realized that she would have to go find him, wherever he was in this strange new world that stood before her. This strange new world that the Sphere and its song had created.

Two

The New World

1

Standing in her room, Olivia finished tightening the belt around her waist, still marveling that her leg was pain-free, and that putting on pants no longer involved pain. She had come back inside to change the clothes she had been wearing. If she was going to go out into the new world and find Adam, she was going to need more suitable clothing for the wilderness than the cotton robe, tank top, and cotton pajama bottoms she had been previously wearing. She chose a pair of durable jeans, a pair of well-worn but comfortable hiking boots, a black tank top, and a red and white flannel for the excursion. The flannel was heavier than what the weather dictates, but she wanted to have an extra layer in case it cooled down. She rolled up the sleeves and left it unbuttoned. Her father had taken her hunting and hiking with him, therefore she had a good idea of what she would need for the wilderness. She grabbed a backpack that she had used when she was younger. It was a skateboard backpack – a style that she had long grown out of from her late middle school and early high school days – but it was durable and had straps that wrapped around the waist and across the chest for an extra secure fit.

With her outfit assembled, Olivia headed to the kitchen and grabbed one of the thermoses that she had previously filled. She tried the water faucet, but nothing happened. She slipped the red thermos into the pocket on the side of her backpack, then opened the zipper to the main compartment. In it, she put a pocketknife, a lighter from the junk drawer in the kitchen, and a few towels, along with the first aid kit that they kept above the refrigerator. She also tossed in some snacks from the cupboard: chips, and a few candy bars. Olivia considered grabbing more but figured she would return before it got dark as she would sleep here tonight. She left the rest of the water bottles there and went to the garage. There she pulled out a large plastic tote with the label "Camping Supplies" written on it. From it she grabbed a compass and a machete in a nylon sheath, which she secured to her backpack. She then dragged a large camping cooler into the kitchen, where she filled it with as many contents of the refrigerator as she could fit into it, including a bag of ice from out of the freezer that had only partially begun to thaw. Concerned about the structural integrity of the house, but seeing that the garage was still intact, she dragged the cooler into the sturdier area, deciding that it was the best place to use as her shelter. Olivia considered the basement for a moment, but did not want the house to crumble down on her. She would have to grab the necessary items to make the garage comfortable enough to sleep in later.

She then headed out the front door, into the wilderness. She stopped for a moment and considered going back to the basement for her father's shotgun. Anxious to find Adam and knowing that she planned on returning to the house anyway, she decided to continue. She had the machete after all, and she figured that it should be enough protection for now. With that decided, Olivia Jane headed out into the wilderness in search of her brother.

2

Olivia's neighborhood was no longer an urban neighborhood, but a deep and overgrown forest. The homes that had once lined the street were mostly collapsed and overgrown with growth, and long grass and brush had overtaken nearly everything. Despite the changes, Olivia was able to push through it with little difficulty. She had to take a wide path around her father's oak tree, which still stood massive and towering in front of the home. As she did this, Olivia passed over what she assumed was the very spot where she had last seen Rick in the front yard, clawing violently at his face. She looked around and listened closely for any signs of him, but only the sounds of birds was in the air.

"Hello," Olivia called out. "Adam?" She stood still and waited for a reply but received none. She decided to press on. The subdivision that had once existed here, had been designed in a large loop, with only a single access road leading out to where it connected to the main drive. Olivia decided to head for the entrance of the neighborhood where a small brown sign read Wedgewood Terrace. From there, she would assess more of the landscape. She made her way around the massive tree and back to what was left of the road her house sat on. It was mostly fractured chunks of the road, spread out with wide gaps of long grass between them. This intrigued Olivia. It looked more like the ground itself under the road had expanded, and in doing so, stretched the road apart into the pieces that she now walked on. She looked around at the rest of the landscape to see if this was true in other places, and indeed it was. The homes, though mostly collapsed, appeared to have much greater distances between them, and were set back farther from the road than they had been before. Was this true everywhere? How did it happen? And how far had this change spread?

Every so often, Olivia would call out again, listening for Adam or anyone to respond. Still, there was no reply. The road continued, though much longer than it had been before. The long grass began to give way to much thicker patches of rough brush that Olivia had to try to go around. Soon, the brush became too much, and Olivia was forced to withdraw her machete from the sheath and cut her way through as she encountered a particularly thick patch. The brush in this spot had grown relatively high, high enough to block her view. She considered going around but found that this patch spread far to the left and the right, like a wall. She traveled the length of this natural fortification for a short distance, looking for either an end or a break. Instead, she found a small hole in it about 3 feet in diameter, enough for her to crawl through. Keeping the machete in her hands, she got down on her hands and knees, and pushed through the hole, emerging on the other side to find the terrain returning to long grass.

From this side, the tall growth of brush indeed was like a natural ten-foot wall. It extended high and thick for as far as Olivia could see. This wall was like a fortification that strongly protected its inner sanctum. The massive tree Olivia had planted stood beyond the wall like the mighty keep of a medieval castle. The hole she had just crawled through was largely covered by the long grass. If Olivia had not just crawled through it, she wouldn't have known it was here at all.

Though she couldn't guarantee that it stretched completely around the tree, and therefore her home and shelter, she felt that it was a significant barrier as well as security against whatever could be out there. If it did stretch completely around the tree, it could be hard to find another way though. Not wanting to lose this entrance, Olivia took the machete and cut off a strip of her flannel shirt at the bottom, it was about four inches long and one across. She then took five large paces to the left of the hole and tied the strip low to the ground. "Five paces to the right," she said softly to herself. Forcing herself to memorize this for when she returned.

3

Olivia tore open a bag of chips and stuffed a pinch into her mouth. She had already eaten one of the candy bars from her backpack and was grateful she had brought them. She had been in such a hurry this morning to look for Adam that she had neglected to eat.

The journey to the entrance of the neighborhood had been longer than she anticipated, with the landscape having been stretched out somehow. But she had finally made it to the old brown wooden sign with yellow letters reading Wedgewood Terrace. She was currently leaning against the sign and resting as she ate. She had partially expected the forest to open beyond the neighborhood; the forest, however, continued. In fact, the forest seemed to go on indefinitely. Still, there was a small clearing here around the sign, it was small, but it allowed for the open sky to be seen. The scene was beautifully tranquil, the grass was soft, and the sun shined down warmly on Olivia, the Sphere hung silently in the sky.

Olivia finished the chips and stuffed the empty bag into her backpack, zipped it up, and then put it back on her back. Securing the straps of the bag around herself. She then grabbed the machete that had been leaned against the sign. She took a deep breath and let it out slowly.

The clearing that started at the sign snaked on like a large path through the trees. This clearing was where the road leading from her neighborhood to the rest of the town started, up ahead was the gas station where she had had her first job, and the clearing wrapped around it, then continued. She knew that there was a small bridge that led over a set of train tracks beyond, though it was out of sight now. Vehicles of varying kinds sat silently amongst the long grass that grew up through the broken and spread apart concrete beneath. Some of the vehicles had their car doors left open, many were piled into the ones in front of them. Though they sat silent now, one could imagine the collision they made with one another when the electricity had been robbed from this world by the Sphere.

Olivia looked up at the Sphere again. It still hung in the sky, motionless. "What are you doing," she quietly asked. Looking down at the empty cars, Olivia wondered where everyone had gone. Just yesterday, or what she assumed was yesterday, she stood in a crowd outside her home. Now, there was no one. La Crosse was home to fifty-one thousand people. Where were they? She called out Adam's name again.

"You," screeched a shrill voice behind Olivia, causing her to shriek with alarm. Olivia spun around to find her neighbor, Sue, standing behind her. Her clothes were torn, ragged and covered with dirt as was her face. She held a kitchen knife in her hand, it was smeared with what looked like dried blood on its blade. Her face was contorted in a hideous snarl, and her eyes were locked on Olivia with an almost palpable hatred emanating from them. The irises of her eyes were a fiery yellow color now, the white around them red and bloodshot. She walked slowly towards Olivia. "You, you sided with him. This was all your doing," she snarled. Saliva dripped from her mouth.

"Sue," Olivia said. Her voice trembled at the sight. "What happened to you?"

"I'm fine," Sue exclaimed. She sounded as if the notion offended her. "I tried to tell my husband that, but he wouldn't listen. Oh, no! They never listen. Well, he listened now. Now, he can only listen!" She let out a cackle that sent shivers down Olivia's spine. Sue was still moving towards her.

"Stay where you are," Olivia asserted, now holding the machete up to block the advancing, crazed Sue. "You're not well, and I don't want to hurt you."

"Oh, my dear. I have never been clearer-minded than I am now," she spread her arms wide open and smiled. "I know what's best. Anyone who can't see that must go! It's for the best. And you, you agreed with that man. You didn't say anything, but you didn't stay to vote for me. You felt guilty! You knew it was wrong! So, you ran! Well, I can make that little mistake go away right now!"

The rabid Sue lunged at Olivia, an inhuman screech escaping her, her bloody knife up in the air and ready to sink into Olivia's flesh. Olivia swung the machete in a swift arch, burying it in her crazed neighbor's neck. Sue fell to the ground; she lay there wheezing for a few moments before falling still and silent. Olivia stood in shock for what felt like an eternity, ragged breaths quickly escaping and entering her lungs.

She may have stayed like that for longer, but the sound of rustling grass and pairs of feet running toward her jarred her out of her shocked state. She pulled the machete from Sue's neck and quickly hid behind one of the protruding brushes.

Two people, whom Olivia did not recognize emerged from the long grass. They, too, seemed to be as disheveled, and crazed as Sue was. One held a clawed hammer in their hands, it was bent and stained with blood. The other held a small hatchet. Both had the same yellow eyes Sue had.

"Why is she here like this," one asked the other. His voice came out in a feral growl.

"I don't know," The other replied. His voice was smaller and more weaselly than his larger counterpart.

"Let me see," a lower voice called from the brush. Out of the long grass, also possessed with the same madness as Sue and the others, stepped Rick. His face bore the deep marks of when he had clawed at it in the yard. The other two cowered down in what seemed like an act of submission to him. He stood over the body of Sue, examining it. He then looked up and scanned the area. Olivia froze but Rick's gaze didn't seem to spot her. "Leave her," Rick finally commanded. "Let's return to the others."

With that said, the three of them ran off into the long grass opposite the clearing from where Olivia hid. With them gone, Olivia let out a long breath. She hadn't even realized that she had been holding her breath this whole time. She looked down at her hands, not surprised to see them shaking.

4

It didn't take long for Olivia to return to the house. She immediately headed to the basement and grabbed her father's shotgun and canvas bag filled with several boxes of shells. The old Mossberg 500 gave her a sense of security after her encounter with Rick and the others. She then proceeded upstairs and grabbed several things from the house before retreating into the garage. Once inside, she shut the door to the house, and pulled a wooden storage cabinet in front of the other door which led outside. That side of the house was overgrown with vegetation, which meant that the door was therefore unable to be opened from the outside, but Olivia was taking no chances.

Darkness had begun to fall, so she lit a candle she had taken from her room. Now, Olivia was sitting on the couch that had been left in the garage. In front of her lay many things. She had grabbed blankets and a pillow from her room and put them onto the couch with a sleeping bag from her closet. She took the rest of the water containers she had filled up before, all the canned food, and a loaf of bread from the kitchen. And several items from the camping storage tote including a line of ripcord, a compass, a small folding shovel, and a small kettle used for boiling water. These things were all now laid out on the floor in front of her, along with the things from her pack and her father's shotgun with the ammunition bag. She surveyed all the items repeatedly.

Olivia couldn't help herself. When she arrived back at the house, shaken by the encounters, she desperately needed to make herself feel safe after what she had seen and done. But now, the task was complete. She had assembled all these things, organized them so that she knew what she had, and now she was alone with her thoughts. The very place she had been trying to avoid by busying herself with the task of assembling her supplies.

What had happened to them? Her mind flashed to Rick in the yard when the Sphere started singing, how he had said something about something being in his head. At first, her thought was that the Sphere had changed them into this. That it had caused this rabid madness. But something that Sue said made her think otherwise. "Oh, my dear. I have never been clearer-minded than I am now," is what she had said. Olivia thought back to the way she was in the yard before, controlling and trying to tell others what to do.

It was as if whatever happened to her didn't change her into something new, rather, it amplified what was already there, it made her hostile and demanded obedience, punishing those who didn't listen to her. And the others? Well, the other two she didn't know. But she did know Rick. If her theory was correct, she could only dream of what he had become.

So, what about her? Had Olivia been driven mad in her own way, and was unable to see it? She still felt like herself - in her mind at least - of course, her leg had been healed. She hadn't become some mad monster either, at least not as far as she could tell. But would she know if she had?

Olivia concluded that she would. After all, Sue described herself as being "clear-minded…now," implying that she was aware of whatever change had happened to her. Olivia wasn't aware of some kind of evil change that happened to her. The thought of killing Sue flashed in her mind. That was self-defense, she didn't want to kill Sue. Though, she had a feeling she would have to do it again - kill in self-defense.

Perhaps she wouldn't. She could stay here in this garage, she had supplies to last for a while, she could hold out here, hidden in the garage, behind the hedge wall. Who knows, perhaps by the time her supplies ran out, help would be here. There had been the military at the La Crosse airport. Surely, they were handling the situation, or at least they would be sending help soon. Besides, Olivia wasn't a warrior. She was a 19-year-old college student. She wasn't cut out for this. Sure, her father had taken her hiking, camping, and hunting, but that doesn't mean she could handle what's out there. Staying here and waiting for help seemed the best thing to do.

What about Adam? She had decided that she needed to find him. What now? Would she abandon him because it was too hard, because it was too dangerous? Olivia hated to admit it, but part of her wanted to. After all, how often did Adam leave her before all of this even happened? And where was he now? Had he not already abandoned her? Just like Mom. Just like Dad.

Olivia cursed herself for that. It wasn't a fair thing to say. Dad didn't abandon her; he didn't have a choice. It was true that Mom did, though. But that didn't mean Olivia herself had to be the same way. No, just because she was hurt, didn't mean she had the right to abandon her brother. Besides, she didn't know what happened to Adam, what made him run. And she didn't care.

Olivia hardened herself in her resolve. It didn't matter, the danger. It didn't matter what crappy way others had treated her. It didn't even matter that it was a strange unknown world out there now, filled with crazy, yellow-eyed people. She would find her brother. She wouldn't be like the people who failed her in her life, she wouldn't be like her mother. Her father's dying effort in this life had been spent making sure his kids were taken care of. That's what she would do.

5

With the new day having arrived, and her backpack filled with supplies, a fresh flannel to replace the torn one, and the shotgun in hand, Olivia set out. She crawled through the brush wall and walked past the spot where she had killed Sue and had seen Rick yesterday. She continued past the sign and into the clearing beyond which should lead to the bridge. If the bridge was still there.

She walked out of the neighborhood, moving down the broken road, collapsed buildings and homes that nature had overgrown were all around. She followed the road, deciding to walk between the cars and use them as cover in case any of those rabid yellow-eyed people like Rick were out looking for someone to attack. She continually scanned the area around her, looking for any signs of danger, and taking care to move as quietly as she could.

The sound of foliage crunching up ahead broke the silence of Olivia's trek. She ducked down and brought the shotgun to her shoulder. The trampling grew louder and closer, Olivia took cover behind a small car and braced for whatever was about to come out of the forest. The noise grew even louder still, as it moved closer to where she was.

Olivia steeled herself for a fight. Her body was tense with worry, her heart pounded fiercely in her chest. The trees began to sway and move now with the sounds, and through the trees, Olivia saw what appeared to be a tree walking through the forest, pressing others out of its way. Then, another tree next to it with the same shape and color moved. For a moment, Olivia looked with bewilderment at this. It wasn't a tree, it had no leaves or foliage on it, it was something familiar, though she couldn't remember what. Beneath the emerging shapes, Olivia found herself looking into two massive black eyes. The behemoth slowly and gracefully stepped out of the forest and into the clearing.

The deer stood at some forty feet in height, its massive, hoofed feet gracefully and expertly stepped in between the cars which were no taller than its first joint. What Olivia had thought were leafless trees were the giant antlers extending from atop its head. The enormous animal strode across the road with confidence and majesty, its ears and tail casually flicking.

Olivia stared up at the creature in wonder and as she did, the air around her seemed to "tingle" in a soothing way. As if the softest and finest strands of hair were gently touching her skin. Small spots of light, like tiny orbs floated in the air around her, silently passing over the landscape. A sort of "magical" feeling surrounded her, she could almost hear music in her mind. Olivia noticed that grass was softly sprouting around her, even pushing its way through the cracks in the asphalt. The grass grew taller and in places it blossomed into beautiful wildflower patches, vibrant with color and beauty. Olivia couldn't help but let out a gasp in wonder.

The deer crossed the clearing and entered the forest on the other side. It casually stepped over a home and disappeared out of view. As it did, the tingle in the air and the small orbs of light passed on with it. The grass and flowers stopped their rapid growth but remained tall and vibrant.

Olivia stayed in that spot for a moment, standing up to stare around in wonder. She then lifted her head to look up at the Sphere and smiled at the beauty it had brought to the world. Yes, there was horror, but there was beauty too.

She resumed her journey, and to the left was a collapsed gas station, and the site of her first job. Kwik Trip, the pride of the Midwest. Up past it, the clearing in the forest narrowed and closed at the foot of the bridge. The still standing bridge rose about halfway up the height of the forest, and the trees formed tight around it. Wrecked and abandoned cars were piled up at its base, as if the cars had made it up part ways, then rolled back into one another when the power was taken.

As she approached the bridge, Olivia became aware of the sound of running water. There had been no running water here before, rather, there were train tracks that ran under the bridge. So, the sound of running water here was indeed strange. Then again, an object from space changing the earth was hardly normal.

Olivia advanced up the bridge and discovered that there was now a river running under the bridge where train tracks had previously been. The water was at least four or five feet deep and moving quickly and powerfully. The river stretched out into the distance as far as Olivia could see. Clearly, the river had carved out the terrain here as the tracks were raised above the surrounding area before the Sphere had done its work. Olivia was grateful for this. It was good to know that there was a source of water near her shelter now that the faucets weren't working.

She reached the top of the bridge, standing directly over the river, and was able to see through the trees for some distance. Normally, one could see the running track of the high school to the left and Central High School just past it from here, but the forest had swallowed them from view. One thing stuck Olivia: the forest did not end. It extended as far as she could see. There were spots and clearings here and there, but for the most part, the city of La Crosse had been engulfed by the wilderness. She looked back at the way she had came and found the same was true in that direction. The forest had overtaken everything. Facing this way, she could see Hedgehog Bluff and Cliffwood Bluff to the left; and to the right, towering over the forest canopy, loomed the massive tree. Her tree. She had put considerable distance between her and it, but it still loomed high above. From her vantage point, it almost seemed to tower above the bluffs, though this could have just been her perspective. It was a beautiful sight, the massive tree, planted by the river.

At the bottom of the bridge, on the other side, was another pile of cars, only this one was much larger, and the vehicles were pointed in the other direction. Olivia was forced to climb over them, and as she did, she felt vulnerable and exposed. Not to mention that it was noisy work. Luckily, a pickup truck had been one of the final vehicles to add itself to the collection, and the tail and box of the truck were easy to climb over.

To the left of the bridge's base was a small red and green building that served as a small strip for businesses. Its large storefront windows had been broken out, and darkness lay inside. Olivia decided to head that way. She figured that if Adam did come this way, he must have stopped for water at the river, and perhaps left a trail or sign here for her to see. As she walked past the building, she became aware of a sound coming from inside. It sounded like a voice, a male voice. She pointed the shotgun into the storefront. "Hello," she called. "Adam?"

There was no reply, but she was certain she had heard a voice from within. It could be Adam, and if it were, perhaps he too was worried and afraid that she was a threat. It was the only lead that she had so far. So, armed with the confidence the shotgun provided, Olivia decided to step in and investigate the sound. She couldn't see inside the darkness of the structure, and again she called out Adam's name. She stepped inside and waited a moment for her eyes to adjust to the dark, she could see that the insides of the place had been crushed and ransacked, though the structure itself seemed intact. Everything within appeared to be covered in some kind of white material as if white blankets or cloth were laid over them. Near the center of the room, on the floor were two objects that appeared to be wrapped in the white substance.

Olivia considered pulling out her lighter to aid in seeing, but did not want to lower the shotgun in case there was something in there. Tentatively, she stepped forward toward the objects, the white substance that covered everything made a sort of crunching sound and seemed sticky on the bottoms of her shoes. As she approached the objects, their shape became clearer to her, and she realized that they were two bodies, wrapped in a white silky substance. Olivia froze. Holding her breath so that she could listen more closely, Olivia became aware that there was a voice in there with her. It was a male voice, whispering in the corner. "Yes, keep coming. Only a little further. Hungry, hungry, always hungry."

In the dim darkness, Olivia slowly realized that a massive shape sat motionless in the corner. At first, it resembled two giant bony hands poised next to each other with their fingers down on the ground. Between these fingers, two massive black eyes reflected light from outside; beneath these two eyes, was a row of four eyes. All of them were fixed on Olivia.

The fingers began to flex, and the shape moved forward. With horrifying clarity, Olivia saw that what appeared to be fingers were massive legs, suspending the body of a giant spider between them. It moved with terrifying speed. Its reflective eyes fixed on Olivia, huge fangs hung beneath the eyes, and two smaller arms around them fidgeted excitedly.

Olivia tried to take steps back, but the beast moved quickly, she pointed the shotgun and pulled the trigger. The weapon let out a loud click, as the firing pin engaged into an empty chamber. Olivia realized that she had never chambered a shell, and quickly cocked the shotgun. But the beast was too quick and was upon her. She fell to the ground, falling with a scream.

"No," she shouted. "Don't come any closer." To her surprise, the beast froze, and then it took a few steps back.

"You?" it questioned. "You can speak, and I can understand you?"

Olivia was frozen with fear for a moment, her mind racing to process what she had just heard, then replied. "Yes, I can speak. I can understand you."

The spider recoiled back, withdrawing its body behind its massive legs. In this posture, the spider looked as though it were frightened.

"How? No one speaks anymore, no one understands. How, how can you speak to me?" Its voice didn't seem to come from its jaws, rather, it seemed to come from inside of it somehow. Its voice started as a demanding shout but seemed to end as though it were breaking with despair. A voice filled with anger and hurt, sounding as if it were on the verge of tears.

Olivia cautiously returned to her feet, still holding the shotgun in her hand, though it was no longer pointed at the spider. "I don't know, she replied. "I just can." A new noise was coming from the spider, who took another set of steps back into the darkness, it was sobbing. This massive spider was crying.

Every single fiber of Olivia's body was screaming for her to turn and flee. To leave this massive and horrid creature behind. However, she found herself, feeling pity for it. "Who are you. Did the Sphere turn you in to this?" she asked. "I want to help you." Olivia had no idea how she would, but she was overwhelmed with concern for the creature.

"Leave me," it uttered in between sobs. "I'm so hungry. It won't go away." It sobbed again, tucking itself further into the dark. "I'm so hungry, always hungry. I don't want to hurt you. I don't want to hurt the others. Go, now."

"What others," Olivia asked. Her fear, now completely gone, thinking of finding Adam. "Are there others? Normal people? Where are they?"

In a dizzying and sudden blur of motion, the spider reared up on its back legs and stretched its front appendages high into the air, filling the space with its massive shape. "I said leave me," it roared in rage, causing Olivia to recoil and take several quick backward steps out of the store. "Go now, go now, leave me, go!"

The desire to flee that Olivia had felt before returned, and this time she heeded its request. Behind her, she could still hear the shouting of the spider as it demanded she flee. She continued running, past the base of the bridge and towards where the riverbank would be. The trees formed around her, and she was running blindly through them, towards the sound of the flowing river. Sorrow and sadness rising inside of her pushed her to keep running blindly. She could feel tears beginning to form in her eyes. She loudly crashed through the forest, giving no thought to the noise she was creating, or the distance she had traveled. Her only thought was to get away to the river.

"Stop," shouted a male voice from in front of her. Olivia came to an abrupt stop at this sound, taking a moment to get herself oriented with her new surroundings. A camp lay before her, a small cluster of tents in a clearing next to the riverbank, perhaps six or seven tents. A fire burned in the center of the encampment and many people were standing around, all now staring at Olivia. Between her and the camp stood a man, taller than her, in blue jeans and a dirty white shirt, pointing a scoped hunting rifle at her.

Three

Not Alone

1

"Stay right there," the man with the rifle commanded. Olivia stayed where she was at the edge of the clearing, still breathing heavily from her run through the woods. She could feel every set of eyes in the camp on her, and a few people were rushing to the side of the man with the rifle. Two of them were armed, one with a pistol and the other with a shovel.

"Good," the man said. "Now, put down the shotgun, and tell me what color your eyes are."

"What?" Olivia asked, confused for a moment by the question.

"Your eyes," the woman holding the shovel next to the man shouted back. "What color are they?"

"They don't look yellow to me," the man with the rifle said to the woman with the shovel. "They look normal to me. Besides, if she was one of them, I think she would be attacking us right now. Not listening to us."

"I'm not one of them," Olivia shouted, now that she understood their fear. She set the shotgun on the ground and held her hands up. "My name is Olivia, and I am human."

"Olivia – is it really you?" a small voice in the camp asked. Olivia recognized the voice before she saw the face. It was Tiffany's, and little Nina stood beside her. They were alive. Despite the rifle pointed at her, Olivia ran around the man and to Tiffany and hugged her tightly. Words could not describe the relief that she felt seeing a familiar face, one that wasn't trying to kill her.

"You're ok," Olivia said, tears of joy now forming in her eyes. For the others in the camp, this display of humanity was enough to dispel their fears. The man with the hunting rifle lowered it down, retrieved Olivia's shotgun - which was still on the ground where she had left it - and walked up to her.

"Sorry for that," he said in a calm voice. Offering the shotgun back to Olivia. "Just had to be sure you weren't one of those yellow-eyed psychos."

"I understand," she replied, taking the shotgun from him. "I've seen them, the yellow-eyed people, it's good to be safe. They're dangerous. Rabid."

"The Rabid," he mused. "That's a good name for them. I'm William, by the way. You can call me Will," he smiled and extended his hand out to her, which she shook.

"I'm Olivia."

Will stood taller than her, at about six feet. He had blond hair, parted on the side. His eyes were blue, and his smile was comforting. He was perhaps in his late twenties and was objectively attractive. "Nice to meet you, Olivia. Welcome to our home."

The woman who had the shovel continued to eye Olivia with skepticism, still clutching her shovel. "Put that thing down, Sheila," the man with the pistol said to her, before walking up to Olivia and introducing himself as Scott.

"She could be faking that she's normal," Sheila growled back at Scott.

"Sorry," Scott said to Olivia. "My wife's just worried. We were hiding in our house when our neighbor came in and tried to kill us. We had known him for years, and always watched the Packer games with him. It's still got her pretty rattled. She'll come around eventually." Olivia wasn't sure.

By now, everyone in the camp was out and watching them, eleven people in total. They looked at Olivia with worry and caution in their eyes, most choosing to observe from a distance. A few even looked on from behind their tents. None of the faces that Olivia saw were familiar.

Olivia turned to Tiffany. "Have you seen Adam," she asked.

"Who is that," Tiffany asked. Olivia realized that Tiffany had never met Adam or learned his name, she had only seen him hit her husband in the stomach with a lead pipe. She also wondered if Tiffany knew what had happened to Rick.

"Have you," Olivia began hesitantly.

"I've seen Rick," she said quickly, a sudden hardness came over her. "He found us in the forest the day after the shaking stopped. Said things to us that I always knew he meant, not just things he said because he was drunk." She looked at Olivia with firm, defiant eyes. "He just has yellow eyes now. That's all." Olivia nodded. She knew she didn't understand everything, but she didn't need to. She was just happy that they were safe and free. "Luckily," she continued. "We ran into Scott and Sheila, and he scared Rick off."

"Took a few shots at him," Scott said. "Didn't hit him, but he ran anyway. Guess he figured he was outgunned."

"We should be careful," Olivia said. "I saw him with two others. He was giving them orders. He may try and come back with more."

Everyone froze for at this. "Giving them orders?" Will asked. "Did they listen?"

"Yes," Olivia said.

Will looked around at the others, who looked concerned. "We didn't know they could be organized," he finally said. "We've only seen them acting alone."

"Maybe it just takes a certain personality," Tiffany concluded bitterly.

Scott and Sheila made their way over to the center of the camp, near the fire. The other survivors approached them and chatted with them urgently, casting wary glances over at Olivia. Scott held his hands up to them in a reassuring manner as he spoke to them. The tension of the group was palpable.

"It's been rough," Will stated to Olivia, as he turned towards her. "Everyone is scared. They have all lost someone, and no one knows what's happening."

Scott's attempts to calmly talk to the group didn't seem to have much effect on them, he eventually gave a shrugging motion to them, then stepped away. Leaving them to chatter with each other fervently.

"We've seen the world transformed into a forest, no electricity, and everyone has encountered the Rabid," Will continued. "How about you? You were running hard through the woods. Did you see something else?"

"Just the Rabid from before," Olivia said, the last thing she needed was to scare these people even more with tales of giant talking spiders. "I was just trying to get as far away from them as I could," Olivia concluded.

Tiffany nodded at this and put her hand on Olivia's arm. "I'm happy you got away safely," she said.

Will didn't say anything for a moment. "Right," he finally replied. "Hopefully they won't follow you here."

"They didn't see me." Will nodded his head, though he seemed to eye her suspiciously.

"Are you hungry?" Tiffany asked warmly.

2

A freshly cooked meal was something Olivia had not been expecting to receive anytime soon. Yet, here she sat, eating a meal of fresh cooked venison steaks chopped into small portions, and a side of boiled potato, all accompanied by a tin cup of water from the river. Will had hunted the deer earlier in the day and had skinned and cleaned it himself. Tiffany had cooked the meat and boiled the potatoes; Nina had helped by peeling the potatoes and putting them into the pot boiling over the fire herself. It had been the first time Olivia had seen Nina smile. The little girl seemed delighted with the whole process, and with her hard work being appreciated by all.

As they were serving the meal to the others, Olivia sat near the edge of the group quietly eating her food. She was concerned with this new development. The people were on edge, scared and unsure. Which was, of course, no surprise given everything. Olivia would be lying if she didn't admit that she did, indeed, want the safety of a group rather than facing the perils of this new world alone. However, she needed to find her brother, and the thought that this group would hold her back from doing so weighed heavily on her. Not to mention that she had already started the relationship with this new group off with a lie. Refusing to talk about the spider with the group, a creature that she knew nothing about, but, had for some reason chosen to be loyal to over these people who were sharing their food with her, was a decision she was wrestling with.

Why? She knew nothing about that creature. Other than it seemed to be in some kind of emotional pain. But, if that was the case, if she truly believed that, then why not tell the others? Surely, they could understand that. Olivia felt overwhelmed with her new situation. She did not know enough. She didn't know what she should do. But she felt as though she had made a critical mistake in holding back the truth about the spider.

She would occasionally catch some of the others in the group looking at her, they seemed nice enough, but the cloud of suspicion could be felt hovering over them. Sheila especially. As hard as it was, and as unsure of the consequences as she was, Olivia felt as though she had made the right choice. They would probably try and kill him if they learned about him, especially Sheila. She was replaying the conversation in her head. The creature had been surprised that they could talk to each other. Perhaps he had tried to talk to other people but couldn't. He also mentioned "the others," presumably that meant these people she was with now. They were near one another after all. He also stated that he didn't want to hurt them. Then again, what if the spider did come and hurt them? He said he was hungry, what if he gave into that hunger and came here - there were two bodies in the store she had found him in after all. If that happened, if he did come here mad with hunger, then that would be on her.

One of the younger people in the group, a high school-aged girl named Melody, was walking around the camp with her cell phone held high in the air. The phone still didn't work, of course, yet that did not stop this young girl from trying. Olivia had met this girl earlier when she was getting her meal from Will and Tiffany. She had given Melody a granola bar from her bag and a can of green beans. Melody had refused to eat the venison that was being offered. She explained that she was a vegetarian and couldn't eat it. "Besides," she stated. "There's so much death and killing happening right now all around us, we totally shouldn't add to the bloodshed." Will did not argue with her, but when he turned to offer the very same bowl to Olivia, Melody asked what vegetarian food he had prepared. That's when Olivia offered her the food from her backpack, worried that an argument in this already tense group would ensue. Olivia shook her head at the memory of this moment.

Olivia needed to find her brother, and to do that, she needed to survive. She couldn't help but feel that this group wouldn't be able to do that. She didn't hate or resent them, but they could be holding her back.

Olivia thought back to her having to kill Sue. Was she becoming someone heartless? Had the Sphere changed her in some way? Here she was, siding with a giant spider, and having little pity for flesh and blood people. No, she did care. She was just overwhelmed, overwhelmed with the complexity of all of this. Besides, Sue was, indeed, killed in self-defense. Hard choices were everywhere in this new world it seemed.

"How is it," Will asked.

"Huh?"

"The food, how is it?"

"Oh," Olivia said, her mind now fully back to the here and now. "It's good, I wasn't expecting a full meal. Thank you."

He sat down on the fallen log that Olivia was seated on next to her. "I was surprised that there were so many deer in the woods," he said, setting his bowl of food in his lap. "After the third or fourth one went past, I decided to get one. I didn't know if we would find other food. The potatoes were random luck, I saw a sack of them sitting in the back of an abandoned car."

Melody let out a loud growl of frustration and put the phone she had been holding into her pocket, sitting back down with a "humph."

"That girl has been trying to turn on her little toy ever since we found her by the bridge," Will remarked. Before shoving a piece of venison into his mouth.

By the bridge, Olivia thought to herself, where the spider lives. So, he must have been talking about these people. If they were by the bridge then they must have walked right by the ruined store he was using as his home. These must be the people he didn't want to hurt. Still, that doesn't explain the two bodies wrapped in webbing inside the store. Who were they? More importantly, had he not wanted to hurt them too? Perhaps that's why he was crying. Perhaps that's why he had urged Olivia to flee. Olivia pulled her mind back to the conversation at hand.

"I guess she thinks she can save us," Olivia replied. "If she can just get a hold of someone."

Will looked at her as though this statement confused him, then simply said, "right." He took another bite, then swallowed before continuing. "Look," he said to her, leaning in with his voice lowered. "I'm just going to be direct with you. I can tell you're hiding something. It's ok, you don't need to tell me. There are lots of weird things in the world now that I don't understand at all. But whatever it is, I need to be sure that it's not something that will hurt these people or put them in danger. I know I just met them yesterday, but it's my job to keep these people safe. So, whatever it is that you are hiding, I need to know if it can hurt them."

Olivia froze for a moment, caught off guard by this direct and pointed question. If she wanted to come clean, this was her moment to do so. But what of the spider, she wanted to help him, but revealing him now would do the opposite of that.

"I've seen some things, and I don't fully understand them. But I don't think they are dangerous, besides the yellow-eyed rabid people, but you already know about them," Olivia conceded after a moment.

Will nodded thoughtfully at this. "Ok," he replied after a moment.

"I have concerns of my own," Olivia said quietly, deciding to take this moment to share her concerns.

"Absolutely," Will replied with a comforting softness in his voice.

"I'm looking for my brother, Adam. We got separated when the Sphere started changing everything. I haven't seen him since. I have to find him, even if it's just to find out if he's dead. I need to do this. I'm concerned I won't be able to do that here. I know it sounds crazy, but this is something I have to do." The words came out in a rush. But Will listened. He waited a moment before replying.

"I understand," he replied. "I don't mean to discourage you. But how will you find him? Everyone here are missing people. They could be dead and buried under this forest, or who knows where. There's also the possibility of him being one of those rabids now. There's no way to know."

"I know that," Olivia quietly snapped. "I have to try. What if he needs my help?"

"The people here need your help. They won't make it without us, and I can't take care of them alone. The most capable person here is Scott, he's a former cop, he has some training. But he doesn't know how to survive out here. He was trying to start a fire with some rocks and wet green leaves. That Melody girl is going to starve out here with a stomach full of grass, and the others are just following the herd hoping that keeps them alive," Will let out an exasperated sigh. "They're going to die. I can't take care of them on my own."

Olivia thought for a second. She knew that Will was right, these people weren't going to make it without help. She considered her options: look for Adam alone, and be alone in this new world, or help here, and keep looking for her brother while staying here with them. It was, indeed, much safer here. That was undeniable. Besides, she had no idea where to start looking for her brother. For all she knew, he ran in the complete opposite direction of where she was going. These people did need her. Tiffany and Nina needed her. She could do both.

"Ok," she finally said. "But I need you to promise me that I can still look for my brother."

Will's face lit up. "OK, tomorrow, we will look together.

Tiffany and Nina walked over and joined them.

"Did you try the potatoes," Nina asked Olivia excitedly.

Olivia chuckled, then took a bite of them while making a sound of approval for Nina.

3

The sound of shouting abruptly woke Olivia from her sleep. She quickly grabbed the shotgun and crawled out of the tent that she was sleeping in with Tiffany and Nina. The fire in the middle of the camp was still burning brightly and cast its rays of light onto the surrounding forest. Olivia quickly spotted Will, Scott, and Sheila standing a few paces away from the fire. As she headed over to them, she became aware that they were staring off at the tree line at a woman, who was standing in the darkness among the trees, staring motionless at the camp.

"Keep your gun on that woman," Sheila commanded Olivia. Sheila's reservations about Olivia seemed to be suspended for the moment. "She tried to kill me."

The woman didn't react to this statement. She continued to stare without moving at them from the darkness, Olivia looked at the others questioningly.

"We woke to the sound of her scratching on our tent. When we came out to see what it was, we saw her. We thought she was hurt, but then she tried to grab Sheila," Scott said.

"She's got blood on her hands," Sheila indicated, holding up her arms to show blood smeared on them from where the woman had grabbed.

Olivia couldn't see the woman very clearly as she was standing in the dark. She walked over to the fire grabbing a longer stick that was burning and carried it over to help her see the woman better. As she approached the woman, the woman let out a moan and took several steps back into the dark, holding up her hands as if to shield herself. Hands that did indeed have blood on them. There was also blood smeared around her mouth. Olivia stopped her advance, but the woman continued to retreat until she stood in the darkness.

Will walked up with his own firestick, he took one step closer than Olivia had, holding up the fire. The woman took another step back, hissing at the fire and baring her teeth like an animal. "Doesn't seem like she's a fan of light," Will remarked.

"Wonder if he is," Scott urged. Pointing to a man who also stood at the edge of the forest in the darkness. This man, too stared soullessly at them.

Will walked a few paces near him with the fire held up again. Just like the woman, the man walked back into the darkness. The man's mouth hung open, and blood surrounded his lips. He had scratch marks on his face and neck. His eyes weren't yellow, nor were hers.

"Those wounds are from someone else," Scott remarked.

"How can you tell," Sheila asked.

"Because the finger marks claw out and not in. Seen enough domestic disturbances to recognize signs of an attacker whose victim fought back."

Rapid, crunching footsteps in the forest caused Scott, Will, and Olivia to draw up their weapons. Another man came running out of the darkness, then stopped abruptly at the tree line, his hands up at the light, he too then retreated into the darkness with the others.

"They're not the rabid," Olivia remarked, just now realizing she had been holding her breath.

"I don't think they're any more friendly," Will replied.

In the darkness of the wood, the sound of yet another one running towards could be heard. This sound was then interrupted by another sound, much larger and much quicker. It moved impossibly fast and intercepted the first sound in the darkness. A hiss and squeal rang out; the sound of a quick struggle drew the attention of even the creatures standing at the edge of the forest.

"What was that?" Sheila questioned, concern filling her voice.

"Sounds like something big just grabbed one of them," Scott replied.

Sheila turned and started throwing logs into the fire. "Then let's keep them away," she said, tossing more logs onto the fire. Olivia started to help and soon the campfire was a roaring inferno, tongues of flames bellowed high into the night. Casting its light onto the surrounding forest, the things retreaded farther away into the darkness.

They stayed up during the night, tending the fire. The things never moved closer. Eventually, dawn came and as the sun rose in the sky, and filled the morning with pale blue light, the things retreated out of sight.

That morning, word about the appearance spread around the camp fast, and Will did his best to answer the concerns and questions of the group. Many took to calling them vampires, though in Olivia's mind that was not a good description. More like some kind of light-sensitive zombies, though they didn't seem like the walking corpses you see in movies. Rather, they seemed like normal people, who had lost their souls or something. By the end of the conversation, the group had taken to calling them Nightcrawlers.

Will did a good job of reassuring the people that whatever they were, the light from the fire held them off. He told everyone that they should have shifts and keep the fire burning bright during the night to keep them at bay, and to be sure that firewood is adequately stacked to keep the fire burning all night. He also stated that as soon as the sun starts to set, everyone must be back in the camp. No one protested this plan. Scott and Sheila took time after the meeting to move their tent closer to the center of camp. It had been on the edge before, and surely sat in darkness at night. Melody and many of the others had slept through the whole night.

Olivia was surprised to find that she wasn't very tired after the events of last night, she had slept for a few hours before the commotion started. Perhaps it was the fact that now there was a new threat out there that was giving Olivia this energy she felt. Not just the yellow-eyed Rabid, but now, deranged vampire zombie people. More perils that Adam had to face as well. Wherever he was.

After Will had finished his speech, Olivia approached him.

"You didn't mention the sound in the woods we heard," she stated in a low voice. "The one that sounded like it got one of them."

Will nodded. "Don't know what it was. Besides, Scott went out into the woods and couldn't find anything. Except for a spot that looks like some brush was thrashed. But no blood, no bodies. Not sure what I would even tell them."

Seems Will was ok with keeping secrets too. In Olivia's mind, the spider was the likely culprit, though she had nothing to back up her idea. She did find some reassurance in the thought that perhaps the spider was eating those things instead of normal people.

"Look," Olivia began. "I know my timing sucks, but..."

"You want to try and find your brother," Will finished for her.

"I'm not abandoning the camp, I will come back," she reassured.

Will shook his head and laughed. "Well, you're crazy if you think you're going out there alone. I'll come with you."

Olivia was relieved to hear this. "Thank you. It doesn't need to be long."

They assembled some gear and set out. Will asked Scott to look over the camp and to make sure that there was enough firewood for the night. Tiffany was worried but understood why they needed to do this. Nina gave Olivia a long hug before asking her to be safe. With that, the two of them set out. Olivia leading the way, she intentionally took them in a direction away from the base of the bridge.

4

The two of them stopped at a tree lying on its side, both feeling tired after their hike through the woods. Taking drinks of water from their packs to cool and refresh their bodies. They had covered a considerable distance. Olivia gazed around at her surroundings. So much had indeed changed. This area, prior to the Spheres' arrival, was a neighborhood with many homes, cars, sidewalks, fences, and roads. Now, however, it was a lush forest with uneven terrain and rock protrusions. Olivia had been looking for homes, and though they passed several that were collapsed and richly overgrown to the point of almost total concealment. There should be far more here than there was. Occasionally they would stumble across scattered piles of house debris that had been overtaken by the forest and its brush, pieces of homes and other signs of a once thriving town were now reduced to pieces and rubble. This lack of evidence of the once-dense neighborhood puzzled Olivia. Where did it all go?

This puzzle had seemed to answer itself when they descended into a low part and Will tripped and fell hard to the ground while they had been making their way to this resting spot. He had caught his foot on a protruding piece of metal. Perhaps in curiosity, or perhaps frustration, Will cleared the dirt away from it to see what it was. He uncovered a roof rack that was still fastened to the top of a red-bodied vehicle of some kind, the majority of which was buried under the ground in rich dirt.

It was at this time that Olivia realized that the forest they were walking in had not grown through the neighborhood that they walked on, but rather, the neighborhood had seemingly sunken into the ground all around them, and the forest had grown overtop of what was here before. Olivia recalled a phenomenon called liquefaction. During an earthquake, sometimes the ground becomes like a liquid, swallowing cars and buildings. It seemed to have happened here.

She wondered how many homes, cars, and people had been buried under the forest beneath them. She also wondered why this had not happened in the neighborhood around her home, her house was still standing, and above ground. She resigned herself to probably never understanding why.

Now, the two of them sat on this log, in a forest, atop the old world. Olivia noticed that Will seemed to be distracted, as if his mind were elsewhere.

"If you want to head back you can," she said, taking another swig of water.

"I'm ok," he replied. "Just wondering if there isn't a safer place for us to move the camp for now. I was considering seeing if Central High School wasn't still standing. Big concrete building with only a few entry points."

Olivia nodded, "that sounds safe enough."

"Only issue is, now we know that we need light to keep the Nightcrawlers away. Without flashlights, we must rely on fire. I don't know if leaving fires burning inside is a safe plan."

"Also, there is no guarantee that the building is even standing. And if it is standing, the Nightcrawlers could be hiding inside of it for all we know," Olivia postulated.

"That's a good point," he remarked. "I noticed that they disappeared this way when the sun came out. Even if they didn't stop moving, they couldn't have gotten very far before the sun would have overtaken them. I wonder if they aren't lurking inside of some of these collapsed buildings we have been seeing."

"I hadn't thought of that," Olivia considered, taking a final swig of water, and returning the bottle to her pack. "I was thinking about taking shelter in one of them if I hadn't stayed with you guys."

"Sounds like I saved your life," Will teased. "Don't worry, you can thank me later."

Olivia smiled and shook her head.

"We do need to find somewhere safer though," Will continued. Seriousness returned to his voice.

"I think I may know of a place," she replied. She told Will about her neighborhood, about the massive tree and the brush wall that seemed to surround it. Will listened with intent and considered it before replying.

"It sounds perfect, but the only issue I can see is a water source. Sounds like we would have to travel some distance away to get water. Rabbids could attack at any time while we got water. That is a big risk."

"I think that risk is going to exist wherever we are. At least there, we have the wall to protect us."

Will gave an expression of agreement. "It sounds like a good possibility. Let me think about it."

Resuming their journey, the two of them found the terrain gradually heading uphill. "Maybe Adam went up here to find a better view."

"Maybe," Will replied. Following Olivia, who had already started picking up the pace to reach the top more quickly. As they approached the top of the hill, which was no higher than thirty feet, they became aware of the sounds of chatter coming from the other side of the hill. Olivia got excited and began to move more quickly. She nearly shouted out Adam's name when Will grabbed her and gave her the "hush" hand gesture. "We don't know who that is," he whispered urgently. Cautiously, they continued up and peered over the top. The voices were clearer now, they seemed harsh and angry.

The hill dipped down a little on the other side, and the forest gave way to a large clearing. In that clearing was a camp, tents and haphazardly assembled wooden structures with tarps pulled over their frames were all around. The largest of these structures was in the center, in front of it was a massive bonfire. Throughout the camp, many people moved to and fro, around forty or fifty of them. They all spoke to one another with harsh words and tones. They all had yellow eyes. Many sat around the fire in the center eating food; above the fire was the body of a person, and pieces had been removed from it.

The sound of soft crying drew Olivia's attention to two large cages that had been roughly constructed out of tree branches. Inside the cages were around a dozen or so people, the looks of either terror or quiet resignation on their faces, Olivia felt her heart skip a beat at the sight. A rise of harsh voices pulled their attention to a group of rabids standing in a small circle away from the fire. There, in the middle of the cluster, stood Rick. They couldn't make out his words, but his body language and demeanor communicated he was giving orders.

"That's Rick," Olivia whispered to Will, unable to conceal the trembling in her voice.

"Let's get out of sight," Will responded. He started to move away, but Olivia put a hand on his shoulder, stilling him. "What," he asked urgently.

"The people in the cages, we can't leave them."

"I know," Will said quickly. "But we can't do it ourselves. We're going to need to get some help. We'll get

Scott, then come back, and see if we can't get them free somehow."

They quietly move down the hill. Once they had put some distance between them and the Rabid camp, Olivia and Will started to run for their camp. Olivia knew they wouldn't be able to keep up this pace the entire way, yet the desire to get there quickly and put the presence of the hostile camp behind them pressed her on.

They were moving so fast through the brush that neither of them had time to react to a man standing in the knee-high foliage. He spun his head around and let out a small snarl, yellow eyes burning with homicidal intensity. Will tried to come to a stop, but his momentum was too great, and he stumbled to an abrupt and unsure stop. The rabid man took advantage of this and thrusted a small blade into his abdomen. Will let out an ugly and guttural gasp, clenching the point of entry and doubling over.

"Will," Olivia exclaimed in a panicked cry. Instincts taking over, she held the shotgun crossways and shoved the Rabid hard, sending him off Will and tumbling to the ground. She then lowered the barrel of the shotgun to the enemy.

"No," Will protested. "Too loud. You'll bring their whole camp to us." Lying on his side and clutching his abdomen, his teeth clenched in pain.

Not thinking twice, Olivia reached her arm back to draw her machete from its sheath on her pack. The Rabid was quickly getting to his feet.

"I must take you to him. Yes, Rage said he was looking for a woman," the rabid growled. "Rage will be happy with me. Not supposed to hurt her, only bring her to him." He lunged up, but Olivia was still struggling to get the machete out. She squealed with fright, realizing that he would be on her. Will, who had gotten off the ground at some point, grabbed the rabid from behind wrapping his arms around his neck, throwing him to the ground. Will raised his hunting rifle up, with the butt of the rifle pointed down, and drove it over and over again into the head of the Rabid. After several sickening impacts on the skull of the downed opponent, it ceased its movement and rambling.

Olivia stood staring at Will, shocked and unmoving. Her hand that was still gripping the handle of the stuck machete was shaking rapidly, making a continual soft tapping sound, her breaths rapid and heart pounding. Olivia looked at the wound on his abdomen, blood was on his shirt. Remembering the first aid kit in her backpack, Olivia pulled herself out of her state of shock and unshouldered her backpack, pulled out the kit, and ran over to Will.

"It's fine," Will said, covering a bloody spot on his abdomen with his hand.

"Stop, show me," she demanded, pulling his hands away.

"Don't, I'm fine," Will said, seemingly unphased. Olivia looked up at him, bewildered, adrenaline still pounding through her veins.

"Will, there's blood. You're not ok," she demanded, getting to her feet. He continued to conceal the wound from her.. "Will," her voice firm. "Show me. Now."

Will looked away and paused for a moment. "Fine," he muttered bitterly. Still not looking at Olivia, he raised his shirt to reveal his abdomen, there was blood smeared in the shape of the wound that should have been. But no wound, only a small pale scar where the wound should be. He dropped his shirt down. Still not looking at Olivia.

Olivia looked in disbelief but collected herself quickly. "The Sphere changed you. You can't die," Olivia half asked, half stated.

Will shook his head, still looking away. "That's not true," he mumbled.

"It's ok, my leg was broken, and in a brace before the Sphere came, and now it's fine, the Sphere changed me too," she reassured.

"You don't understand," he said quickly, the firmness in his voice taking Olivia by surprise. "I did die." He finally looked at Olivia, uncertainty in his eyes. As though he were afraid to say more, but desperately wanted to. "I woke up here, Olivia. I woke up to this new world. I died of lung cancer in a hospital room in 1993."

Four

Rescue

1

"I was born in 1931," Will started slowly. "Which, until a day or two ago, wasn't a strange thing for me to say. It was just my father and me. He drank a lot, hit a lot. I couldn't wait to get out of that house when I was growing up. Truth be told, I was almost relieved when they drafted me to Korea. War seemed better than being in that house. Even when we were trapped at Chosin, I thought to myself "I've been trapped before, the enemy just looks different now. At least I can kill my enemy over here." Will shook his head bitterly. "19 years old, grateful that I could kill. I was a very different person when I left Korea, after the Battle of Chosin. I was angry. But it didn't matter, everyone was celebrating us when we got back, that is, everyone but my father. He stayed away from me, and I stayed away from him."

Will looked down, then away again. His face seemed wrecked with shame, unable to look Olivia in the eye. "I met a woman, Betty. She was patient, kind, and beautiful. We had a daughter, Sarah. She had the sweetest laugh." Tears welled up in Will's eyes, "But it didn't matter how wonderful and perfect they were. How much she supported me, and how precious Sarah was. I couldn't stop drinking, couldn't stop being angry over absolutely nothing. Whenever I would get angry or sad, I would drink, and the more I drank, the angrier and sadder I became. She would be the most wonderful wife, then do one thing that angered me, and I would fly off the handle like the world was ending. Like all the other wonderful things about her didn't exist."

"One night, I got drunk. I don't remember what happened after. But I woke up to an empty house. I found a note from Betty. She told me she couldn't do it anymore, that there were many things she could forgive, but she couldn't forgive what I did. She said she had gone to her mother's, and that she would only see me if I could stop drinking for one year. I never stopped. And I never saw her or Sara again. I still don't know what I did," Will shook his head bitterly again, looking up to the sky, fighting the tears back. "That's not true, I know exactly what I did. I became my father." Will let out a harsh breath, composed himself, and continued.

"Years and years went by, drinking, smoking, working. No purpose or value. I never tried to stop, never tried to reach out to Betty or Sarah. I got the lung cancer diagnosis and was told that it was the smoking that did it. Before I knew it, I was looking up at the ceiling of a hospital room in La Crosse. Struggling to breathe. No one came to visit me. Can't say I blame them much. In the end, it was me and a nurse whose name I didn't know. The morphine made it not hurt so much. My final thoughts were that my life was a failure, I failed my family. I wish I could have been enough of a man to at least see my little Sarah one last time. There was a phone next to my bed. I could have tried, even just to say sorry for being the worthless wretch that I was. Tell them that they were wonderful and that I was the problem. But I didn't. In the end, I was a failure of a father, just like mine was. My life was a waste. I was almost happy to die. Happy for the failure to be over. I was 58 years old." He closed his eyes for a moment, then looked up at the Sphere, silently dangling in the air.

"I woke up in darkness. Like letting yourself float on the surface of the water in a river. I saw the Sphere above me. I felt it speak to me, not in an audible voice, but in a pressing conviction in my heart. It doesn't talk, it pushes its truth onto your heart."

"What did it say," Olivia asked, she had been sitting on the log next to Will, and her voice was soft and understanding. He was bearing his soul in ways that most people never will in their lives.

"It told me that it wanted me to go back," he said, his words were slow as if he were trying to translate a language foreign to him. "But I would have to do something. That I would have an important task. As it spoke, there was light all around, I was suspended in this vast, endless void of white light. I pressed into my heart and asked if I would do this. I told it: Yes."

"The darkness came rushing back to me, and everything around me was shaking. I was in a small space and could feel the space I was in moving with me inside of it. I pushed hard and fell to the ground. I fell out of a coffin, my own coffin. The ground around it had been pushed up and the wooden box I had been in hoisted up into an almost vertical position. I was in the cemetery a few miles north of here. The forest greeted me, rather than the town that I knew, and up above was the Sphere. Looking down on me as if to say: "Ok Will, time to get to work.""

"I felt like I was being led to walk in a certain direction, so that's what I did. It was the same pressing of truth on my heart that I had felt before. So, I obeyed, like the soldier that I used to be, I marched on. I found a rifle in the back of a truck, that's when I saw my reflection in the mirror. I was the same age I had been when I met Betty, when we had Sarah. I had to get rid of the clothes I had on, the suit they buried me in was cut up the back, falling off of me. I suppose it's easier to put clothes on a dead body that way. I kept on. That's when a rabid found me, I didn't know what it was. It got the best of me. But my wounds healed. After I killed it, I took its clothes,"

"I kept following the calling, kept on walking in the direction I was pushed to. I heard shooting and ran to help. That's when I found Scott and Sheila, they had just found Tiffany and Nina. The shots were when they chased away Rick. When I saw them, I felt the truth pressing in my heart again. It told me to keep them safe."

Will looked at Olivia, a stern determination was in his eyes. "I don't know why it picked me. But it did, and it brought me back for a reason: to protect these people. I failed in my first life, then it came and gave me a new one. I will not fail them."

Olivia paused for a moment, then put her hand on Will's shoulder. "I think that's why the Sphere came," she said, her voice filled with comforting reassurance, "to make the world a better place, and I think we are supposed to help it. We have a part to play."

Will nodded. "Let's help those people in the rabids camp, then get our people to safety. Then, we will find your brother."

"Ok," Olivia replied. "But first. There's something I have to tell you. You told me your secret, so I'll tell you mine. We need to go to the base of the bridge. There is someone there who may be able to help us."

2

They stood outside the small, broken-down shop where Olivia had seen the spider only the day before. Though Will did indeed trust Olivia, and her assertions that she felt they could trust this creature, he still appeared to be hesitant.

"So, it's a big spider? He asked.

"Yes," Olivia replied. "But he can speak."

"Right, and only you can hear him?"

"Will, I need you to trust me on this."

"I trust you; I do have reservations about the itsy-bitsy spider who has dead people in his house and talks about being hungry."

"He isn't itsy-bitsy."

"That's not helping."

Olivia rounded the corner of the store and stepped inside. "I'm back," she said loudly into the store. "I have someone with me, don't worry, he is a friend." Only silence answered her. She took a few steps further in, stopping at the place where she had fallen the day before. There, the two bodies, wrapped in spider silk still lay, but a third had joined them now.

"I thought you said there were two before," Will asked, the concern in his voice clear.

'I think this may be the nightcrawler from last night," she replied.

"We don't know that for certain," Will retorted.

"You can't die, Will," Olivia replied.

"True, but I don't want to spend forever wrapped up in a spider web being eaten over and over again either."

Olivia shuddered at the thought of that. "Never thought of that."

"I thought of that when I first saw the river, how horrible it would be to be trapped underwater, drowning for eternity."

Olivia agreed. "Spider!" She shouted. "We could use your help with something!" Again, no reply came. Peering into the dark, she walked as far back as she could. But found the place to be empty. "He's not here."

"We should go, we don't have much time. We still need to get Scott and then head there, help the people somehow, then get back before nightfall."

The thought occurred to Olivia that the nightcrawlers would make things very difficult to get back to camp with. Especially if they had the people from the rabid camp with them.

They walked away from the store, and towards camp, on the same path Olivia had run the day before.

"I have a question," Will remarked.

"Ok," Olivia replied, his tone seemed strange.

"What is that thing that Melody keeps trying to turn on?" Olivia let out a small laugh. "I'm serious," Will laughed as well. "Iv heard about those Gameboy things, is that what it is?"

"It's a phone," Olivia remarked. "Well, they are more like computers now. It's not just for phone calls, you can send people messages, video call them, watch videos and get on the internet with them."

"Can we keep my age a secret for now," Will asked, his voice lowered.

"Can we keep the spider secret for now," Olivia asked.

"Speaking of Melody," Will said, looking over to a spot in the woods off to their right. Melody sat on the ground, she seemed to be talking to herself with a low and hush voice, she held her phone in her hand flat on her palm. Will removed his backpack and carried it pressed against his side, so that the tear and bloodstain of his shirt would be concealed.

"Melody," Will called out, startling the young girl.

"Yes, what, what," she replied awkwardly. She had the appearance of someone who had been startled, or as if she had been caught doing something she shouldn't have.

"Are you ok," Olivia asked.

"Mm-hmm," Melody replied, not looking at them.

"Did you get your phone working," Will asked.

"Nope," she said, then abruptly walked away back to camp.

Will and Olivia exchanged questioning glances with one another.

3

"A whole camp of them, and you want to go galloping in on some kind of rescue mission," Sheila asked incredulously.

"We can't just leave them there. Sheila." Scott's voice was a practiced tone of calm and reassurance.

"We have a plan to distract them and keep their eyes off the cages so we can sneak the people out," Will reassured. Will had discreetly changed out of the torn white shirt and now had on a clean grey shirt.

"It's a good plan," Scott remarked, both to Will and to his wife.

"Nothing about going into a camp of crazy murderers is a good idea," Sheila rebutted. "We should just go straight to the safe place by the tree Olivia told us about."

"We can't just leave those people," Will said. The plain way he spoke seemed to communicate frustration under the surface. "What if it were you in the cages, would you want someone to come for you?"

Sheila looked down at the ground. The frustration on her face was clear. "If we are going to do this it has to be now," Scott asserted. "Before the night falls, it's almost noon now and we don't want to be trapped in the dark with those things."

Olivia, Will, and Scott grabbed their weapons and prepared to head out, taking only the bare necessities with them. Scott and Sheila had a moment of intense discussion by their tent that Olivia was unable to hear, but she did see it end with a long and sincere hug. Scott kissed her on the forehead, and she clung to him tightly before he joined Will and Olivia on their way out of the camp.

"She's had to watch me walk out our door and work as a cop for years," he said to them. "Always worried I wouldn't come back. We thought those days were behind us I suppose. This is scarier, but she can handle it."

"I wish I could tell you that you can stay back," Will replied.

"It's ok, I want to help. I may be older, but I'm not dead."

Will was quiet. "Besides," Scott continued. "Someone has to watch out for you two kids."

They made decent time getting to the rabid camp, Olivia wasn't entirely sure of how long, but the sun was only just starting its descent away from the high point in the sky. Still, she wanted to be sure of what time they were looking at.

"What time do you think it is," she whispered.

"After two," Scott whispered back.

"Good, that should give us time to get them and make it back before night."

The three of them crouched on top of the small hill next to the Rabid camp, where Will and Olivia had spotted it before. The camp appeared very much the same way that it had been a few hours ago. Olivia quickly counted the people in the cages and found the number to have remained the same. She was relieved. The rabids in the camp seemed to be walking and sitting idly in a casual manner as if it were just another day for them. The body of the person still hung above the fire in the center.

The three of them silently moved down to the base of the hill, out of sight.

"All right let's do this quickly," Will said. "Olivia, you circle around the back of the cages, Scott and I will circle around to the other side of the camp and start our own fires about one hundred feet apart, that should get their attention. Got the flint I gave you, Scott?" Scott pulled a flint and striker set out of his pocket. "Good, as soon as the fire is lit, move immediately. It shouldn't take long for them to notice the smoke and come and investigate. Just remember to move quietly when you get away. Olivia, keep the survivors calm until the camp is distracted, but figure out a way to get the cages open. When those in the camp react to the smoke, try to get the cages open. Scott and I will circle back and meet you at the cages, unless you get them out before we get there; then just head back to our camp and we will meet you there. Everyone got it?" Olivia and Scott nodded quickly. "Good. Stay quiet and stay safe." They departed to their designated areas, Olivia moved silently around the camp to the left, while Scott and Will moved together to the right.

Despite how quiet Olivia was doing her best to be, every footfall in the brush seemed louder than the one before. The sound of Olivia's pounding heart filled her ears, she feared that others could hear it as well. The area surrounding the camp was low, so Olivia was able to keep the rising ground between her and the line of sight of the camp, giving her room to move quickly. From above, the harsh and quick words of the Rabid reached her, though she couldn't make out exactly what was being said. Regardless, she still shuddered at the cruelty and malice in the voices.

A voice sounded off near Olivia up on the hill and caused Olivia to take cover behind a small bush that was in her path. The voice belonged to a woman, though Olivia couldn't see her from behind her hiding spot. The voice didn't seem to be saying any discernible words, rather unintelligible snarls and murmurings, there appeared to be no responding voice, Olivia speculated that the Rabid woman was muttering to herself. It wasn't long before the woman moved off, taking the sound of her hateful muttering with her.

Olivia knew that she could go, that she should go, but fear left her paralyzed. She remained crouched behind the bush for several moments, breathing heavily and shaking with fear. *Get up, Olivia.* She tried to command herself in her mind, that they needed her and were counting on her. Still, fear kept her in this position. She wasn't sure how long she stayed in the position, wasn't even sure if she could move again. A greater fear eventually pushed her out of that spot, the fear of leaving the people in the cages, as well as Scott and Will fending for themselves. She was needed. People would die if she didn't move now.

She got her feet moving again, afraid that her courage would leave her again. Her mind was a tumult of emotions: fear, anxiety, worry, and now - indignation. Why, she thought to herself, still staying low under the camp's line of sight. Why has this burden come to her? I'm a college student, she thought to herself incredulously. Nineteen years old. Now, I'm engaging in a rescue mission with an ex-cop and a ninety-year-old dead Korean War veteran. She looked up to try and find the Sphere but couldn't spot it through the tree cover. A few days ago, she felt that it was here to make the world a better place, she felt it deep, deep in her bones. But now, considering all that had happened. She wasn't so sure.

She now had arrived to the edge of the forest, behind the cages that sat on the edge of the hill, and the edge of the camp. Luckily, this meant that the area immediately behind the cages was still covered by the forested downslope around the camp, and therefore, Olivia could remain out of sight; even as she tried to cut the back sides of the cages free while out of sight.

The cages were constructed out of long branches and the trunks of smaller trees, all held together by long nails and tightly wrapped and tied ropes of various kinds, including ripcord and twine. This was good, Olivia had a knife on her that would let her cut the ropes with relative ease to make a way for the captives to crawl out. Inside the cages she could see the people, most of them were lying on the dirt floor of the wooden prison, their clothing was dirty, and many had bruises and cuts on their faces and arms. Olivia counted twelve in total, five in one cage, and seven in the other.

"Psst. Down here," Olivia called quietly to the nearest cage. No one moved at first. She called again, a little louder than before. A man in a flannel shirt turned his head towards her. She immediately held up one finger to her lips in the universal signal of, "quiet or you'll get us killed." The man's eyes wet wide with hope and excitement, though he kept quiet. "We're going to get you all out of here," Olivia whispered to him, pulling out the knife from its holster on her waistband and going to work cutting through the ripcord.

The others in the cages slowly started to come alive, Olivia felt overwhelmed with emotion as she saw all their faces turn from acceptance to their fate, to hope and anticipation. Many started to softly cry and whisper "thank you" under their breath. There were children in the other cage, and the woman holding them shushed them. They were elated silently in their newfound hope, but also cast worried glances around the camp. Terrified that their salvation would quickly be snatched away from them.

"I'm Travis," the man in the plaid shirt said to Olivia, who was well on her way to cutting a hole large enough for them to start to crawl through. "I can't tell you how happy we are to see you."

"Olivia," she replied, finally finishing the hole, and using the strength of both of her arms to pull it open. Travis immediately pushed his way through, then took Olivia's place holding it open while she headed over to the other cage to repeat the process.

"Thank you, thank you, thank you," the woman holding the two children whispered emphatically, tears streaming from her eyes. "They were going to slaughter us like cattle. That's what this cage is for. They put the useful people in the other cage."

"What does that mean?"

"The doctor, and other people strong enough to work for them go into that other cage, the rest of us are for food."

Olivia found herself cutting harder and faster after hearing this, partially blocking out the image of the body above the fire from her mind.

"One of them is coming," an urgent voice from inside the cage whispered. Everyone, including those in the other cages, went perfectly still. Olivia stopped her cutting and squatted down, peering through the chaotic construction of the cages.

A rabid woman, possibly the one that Olivia had heard before from behind the bush, was walking some distance off the cage. She wasn't currently looking at the cages, but was walking towards them, possibly to check on them, or even to take one of the captives out. As she approached, Olivia could hear the same hateful murmuring from before, only clearly now. "Mine, mine, the job was mine. He was a man, yes, a man. That's why they picked him. It should be me, me. Kill him, I will. Kill him, take his power, make it mine. Make everyone listen to me. Power for me, job for me." The woman looked at the cage, and briefly looked away for a moment, then snapped her head back, locking eyes with the cages. Her face seemed confused for a moment. Behind the woman, Olivia could see two trails of smoke ascending into the sky, but none of the camp seemed to have noticed it yet. Olivia cursed under her breath.

The sound of a gunshot rang out far on the other side of camp, every head and set of eyes in the camp turned towards the source of the sound. For half a moment, no one moved. Two more shots, both in quick succession, rang out from the same place. The entire rabid camp roared with a chaotic blend of screaming, shrieking, and the horrid hateful chatter of them shouting to one another. All the rabids in the camp, including the woman who had been looking only a few moments ago, raced for the source of the sound.

Deep concern filled Olivia's mind. *What had happened, that wasn't the plan. Why had they fired shots?* Two more shots rang out, this time, a little to the left of where the first had been, still on the other side of the camp, yet farther away from the rally point on the hill.

Even though this wasn't the plan, it still had the same result. The camp's attention was all diverted to the opposite side, and Olivia was free to finish cutting open the second cage. The children the woman was holding came out first, then her, and then the others. Travis came over and aided in getting everyone out. They all followed Olivia, around the camp to the base of the hill where they had all agreed to meet. Will and Scott were not there.

"Ok," Olivia said to herself, remembering the plan. "We head back to our camp," she said to Travis, who had stayed next to her. The sound of quickly moving feet drew Olivia's attention to see Will scrambling to them from the direction he and Scott had come.

"They got Scott," he exclaimed, before moving up the hill. Olivia followed him, leaving the survivors at the base of the hill. When they got to the top of the hill, they were in a low crouch position, Will unshouldered his hunting rifle and began scanning the camp and its far edge with the scope. Olivia dug in her bag for her small binoculars. Travis joined them.

"What's happening, shouldn't we get out of here," Travis whispered urgently.

"They've captured one of ours," Will replied.

Olivia scanned the edge of the camp, at first seeing nothing. A large group of rabid came out of the camp, whooping and hollering in a display of elation and victory.

"Looks like they are coming back," Olivia reported. Will lined the group up in his sights. More rabid came out of the forest's edge, the group was sparse at first, but it bulged out into a large, concentrated group. Atop the group, held up in the air, was the body of Scott. Olivia let out an audible gasp and had to choke back tears. Scott was clearly dead; a large wound of some kind bloodied his face. To the side of the group walked Rick. In one hand he held a bloody hatchet, in the other hand he held Scott's pistol.

The mob of rabid began chanting together. "Rage, Rage, Rage, Rage!" Their cruel voices and snarling speech melded together in a horrifying sound that made Olivia's skin crawl. They carried the body to the large building in the center of the camp and entered its large entrance. Scott's body was still hoisted above. Their chanting sounded like a horrible drone in the background, fading away as Olivia and the others retreated to the safety of the camp.

Five

Darkness

1

The evening had descended on their home base, and the camp's fire burned high into the night sky, pushing back the darkness around, and three smaller fires had been created at the edges of the encampment to make an additional perimeter of light to cover the new arrivals. There were many new faces, and with that, many more mouths to feed.

Will had prepared the last of the remaining deer meat, and Tiffany and her little helper Nina had been busy cooking it up and preparing it - although Nina was keeping an eye from afar on the other new kids that had joined their band of survivors. Olivia pitched in all the canned food that she had remaining in her pack to help after it became evident that the remaining potatoes would run out quickly during the meal.

The mood of the night was mostly one of celebration and gratitude, these twelve people were prisoners who had been imprisoned and facing certain death or slavery only hours ago. They were now free and eating a meal prepared by people who welcomed and embraced them, there were smiles and handshakes all around and people were eating a fresh warm meal. The lightheartedness of the moment was remarkably refreshing.

Of course, underneath it all, was the sadness of Scott's loss. It hung in the air silently now, and though the survivors of the rabid's camp couldn't feel it as much as the others, everyone was at least subtly aware of it. For Sheila, it was not subtle. When the party had returned from the woods, she had been standing at the edge of the camp, waiting for her husband. Olivia was sure that she would never forget the sound of her screaming when Will approached her and told her what had happened. She had to be taken away by some others and brought to her tent when she began hitting Will and cursing at him. That had been hours ago, and she still had not come out for food.

Still, in that time, the two groups had met one another and bonded over the current circumstances, figured out sleeping arrangements, and were largely excited about the prospect of moving across the river and to a safer place. Once the food began to be prepared, and the smell of freshly cooked venison, cooked potatoes, and heated cans of miscellaneous food filled the air, the camp came alive with an energy that hadn't been in it before. Hope and laughter were even being heard here and there in the camp. One of the older men from the cages had mentioned that he played guitar, and a member of the camp produced a classical-style acoustic for him. After a little tuning, the sound of music filled the air, and a merry and hope-filled tone that had been dead for days floated around the camp. True, there was morning over the loss of Scott, but there was a celebration of life as well.

Olivia didn't know how to feel. She mostly hated the mix. She felt concerned when the guitar came out and the music began. In the tent near one of the three perimeter fires, Shelia was having the worst night of her life, and the sound of joyful music could only have hurt her spirits even more. On the other hand, Olivia was not about to tell the people who had just been liberated from certain death that they needed to halt their joy. Still, Olivia herself couldn't shake this feeling and rather chose to busy herself with taking care of those who were there.

Donating the canned food from her bag was just the beginning of this process. She now found herself aiding the new doctor in wrapping up cuts, scrapes, and other injuries, she gave him her first aid kit and helped here and there by holding bandages in place as he wrapped them. Surprisingly, most of the issues were just this, minor wounds. And, as it turns out, healing was not limited to her and her leg.

"Still no sickness or infections," Dr. Travis - as everyone in the camp now affectionately called him - commented. "Many of the injuries the yellow-eyed freaks made me look at should have had signs of infection. And still, none of them did. Mr. Gregofski over there - that's the one playing the guitar - stated that he was in the final stages of cancer and had decided to go home to die. After the Sphere came, all his cancer symptoms were gone. Personally, I saw no evidence that it had ever been there. Hell, I had a knee that gave me issues for years. And now," he gave his right knee a good slap. "Nothing." Olivia took a moment to tell him about her leg that had been in a brace only a few days before. Dr. Travis simply nodded in approval. "That only proves my hypothesis," he concluded. "No sickness, infection, or disease, and it seems that previously existing injuries also seem to be remedied by our new friend in the sky. Still, we don't want to throw away proper infection protocol, just in case." He pulled off a pair of rubber gloves from the first aid kit.

Olivia noted to herself that Dr. Travis said our friend in the sky, as in singular, not as in multiple beings inside of a spaceship as the news and the populace had been saying all along before the power went out and before the Sphere had changed the world with its song. Given that they were already discussing the impossible, and that they were all living in it now, Olivia decided to ask a question that had been silently nagging at her. "You think it's a single entity, and not a spaceship filled with aliens," she asked, finishing up wrapping the sprained wrist of the mother who had tearfully thanked Olivia for getting them out of the cage.

Dr. Travis paused for a moment, taking a moment to find the right words. "Yes," he finally said. "I can't explain it, but I feel as though I somehow just know. Knew that it's some kind of lifeform or creature, or something."

"I felt the same thing too," Olivia commented.

The mother, whose name was Megan, nodded. "I thought the same thing too, and thought it was just me. But then my daughter, Sophie also started to call the Sphere an "it," rather than "them.""

Olivia considered saying that Will also believed that it was a singular being, but held this detail back. He didn't want her to share his story.

"Not sure if that is reassuring, or more terrifying," Dr. Travis remarked, rubbing sanitizer into his hands. Olivia did still feel, in her heart, that the Sphere was good, but kept this comment to herself.

Finishing the wrap on Megan's wrist, Olivia scanned the crowd to see if there were any more people waiting to be seen by the doctor and was relieved to find that there were none. She did, however, spot Melody walking away from the center of camp where the food distribution was happening. Olivia hopped up and grabbed the granola bars from her pocket. She had set them aside and was saving them to give to Melody so she wouldn't have to worry about her vegetarian diet again this evening.

"Melody," Olivia called out to her. As she turned to face her, Olivia noticed that Melody was holding a bowl of freshly cooked venison in her hands, in fact, Melody was actively chewing and already had another piece skewered on the end of a fork. "Oh," Olivia remarked. "You're eating venison."

"Yes," Melody replied, shoving the piece into her mouth hungrily. "I was so hungry; I hadn't eaten anything for lunch." Olivia was taken back by this for a moment, as well as by other things about Melody that seemed different. She had bags under her eyes as if she hadn't slept for some time, but the most alarming difference was her voice. It seemed that much of the inflection that made her voice distinctively hers was missing. Her hair was different as well, it was tucked behind her ears and not hanging down as it had been before. Most surprising to Olivia, her phone was nowhere to be seen.

"Oh, Good, well let me know if you need anything," Olivia said, unsure of how to react to the subtle changes.

"Thanks," she replied. She then, abruptly, walked away and sat with a group of others who were seated next to one of the perimeter fires. Olivia stood, bewildered, before noticing that Sheila had appeared outside of her tent, and was sitting alone, staring at the different people who were around.

Olivia, overwhelmed with compassion and pity for her, went to the serving station, got a bowl of food with a side of green beans, and brought them to her. Sheila glared at Olivia as she approached her.

"I brought you some food, Shiela, I thought you might be hungry." Sheila smiled bitterly, stood up, and took the bowl from Olivia.

"It's all your fault," Sheila calmly said, looking Olivia in their eyes. "I just wonder if you know that."

Olivia had wondered if a comment like this would come, and now that it had, she found herself surprisingly calm. She had chosen compassion long before walking over here, and wouldn't abandon it now. "I know you're hurt, and angry, Sheila. We all are, none of us wanted this to happen."

Sheila scoffed loudly, drawing a few sets of eyes from the camp. "You know that, hm?" She remarked, bitterly. "What the hell do you know?" her voice was now a raised accusation causing Olivia to take a step back. Sheila advanced. "I knew there was something wrong with you the moment you came running into our camp, we should have shot you right then and there."

Will appeared at Olivia's side, "That's enough Sheila."

"Oh, of course, you come running to her aid," the venom still fresh in her voice. "Cute little girl comes running into camp and you go off into the woods with her. Good trade for you, trading my Scott for her!" The camp had fallen silent now and all eyes were on the conversation. "She did this," Sheila continued, an accusatory finger out now for all to see. "She came and dragged you off to the woods, what did you do to him? I know it was you!"

"It wasn't her fault," Will protested. "She wasn't there, she was helping free these people."

"Then what happened?"

"I don't know," exclaimed Will. "He must have stumbled on one of them by accident. He lit his fire, just like we had planned, perhaps he alerted one closer to him than he realized. The shooting started and he was swarmed before I could do anything. Either way, it wasn't Olivia's fault." At some point, Tiffany had come up alongside Olivia and put her hand on the inside of her arm. This seemed to infuriate Sheila.

"You weren't watching him, you abandoned him for her. And now all of you are doing the same," she was shouting now, her finger lashing out at everyone around her. "You all, you all did this. If we had just listened to me, then he would still be alive, we would all be safe. Now, they will come for all of us because you took them from them!"

Olivia felt an anger boil inside of her. "If we hadn't then all these people would still be with the Rabid, waiting for their turn to die."

"I don't care, I don't care!" Sheila shouted, her finger waving and pointing at everyone around her again. "All of you should be back there, all of you, I would send you all back in a heartbeat if I could." As she finished her last sentence, her finger fell upon Megan, who stood silently watching, clutching her two children to her. Sheila froze at this. A mix of anger and shame on her face as her glaring eyes darted around at everyone, tears filling her eyes. Without another word, she turned and disappeared into her tent.

It took a few moments, but eventually, everyone turned and went back to their meals. No music played, no laughter was heard, only soft talking and the sound of people adding logs to the fires that kept the darkness at bay.

2

A lack of sleep and the need to relieve herself drove Olivia out of the tent she and Tiffany shared, only now it had Megan and her two kids as well. Olivia had sacrificed her blanket to keep the kids covered and had to resort to using her pack as a pillow, and her flannel as her blanket. Neither was working well and when her bladder decided to protest along with her back and neck, she abandoned the cause of sleeping temporarily.

Grabbing a torch from the fire and letting one of the people that Will had put on guard know what she was up to, Olivia headed to the perimeter of the forest and took a few steps in, holding her torch nice and high so that she could be sure to ward off any nightcrawlers that could be around. Not waiting to be too far into the dark, but not waiting to be seen by the camp, Olivia took to a spot behind a tree.

She finished what she set out to do, but as she was getting ready to return, she found that she couldn't. Her mind raced and pedaled on rather than her body. She found herself consumed with thoughts of Scott, of him surrounded by the Rabid, fighting alone. She thought of the person whose body was above the fire in the rabid camp: *what had happened to them, did they suffer, did they have a family, where were they, did they suffer the same grisly fate?* She thought of Sheila, she wasn't angry at her, but she was hurt by her reaction, and was saddened by her pain at the loss of her husband. She finally thought of her brother, Adam. Where was he in all this madness? Had he just abandoned her? Tossed her down the basement stairs as if she were some unwanted responsibility that he was thankful to get rid of so he could take care of himself. Was he dead in this endless forest somewhere, buried under the dirt to never be found, leaving her to wander the earth looking for him to no avail for the rest of her days? Or was he roaming around, one of those people standing in the darkness, or was he Rabid, yellow-eyed, and hunting people down? Even more haunting was the possibility that Olivia may never know.

Tears filled Olivia's eyes as the emotional pressure of all her thoughts and fears bubbled up, she soon realized that they were too great and that she could not hold them in. She took a few steps away from the tree and fell to her knees, deep, deep sobbing of uncontrollable intensity overtook and poured out of her. Like a vast dam that had been holding back an ocean of rage, hurt, and isolation finally broke and the great deluge of everything she had experienced over the past few days overtook her. She curled into a ball, now sobbing with full intensity.

"Adam, Adam," she moaned through the tears. "Adam, Adam, where are you?" She knew that she should stay quiet, that there could be dark and evil things in these woods, but nothing could hold back all that was coming out. "Dad," she whimpered. "Daddy, why did you have to leave?" The night offered no response. She thought of her mother but found that it only made her angry. Still, the emotions were subsiding, and she soon found herself exhausted and the pressure relenting.

She wiped the tears from her eyes, concerned that others would see and become concerned themselves, or that she would worry the two mothers who had been through enough in her tent. She got up, grabbed the torch from where she had left it, and was preparing to head back to the camp when a voice in the darkness called out to her.

"You," the voice called. "You. Can you hear me?"

Olivia turned her torch towards the direction of the voice, to find a very familiar pair of eyes looking back at her from the inky black. Two large ones next to one another, and a row of four underneath. Beneath them the small appendages called pedipalps fidgeted silently, framing the massive fangs that Olivia had seen before in the store by the bridge. "You can. You can hear me, can't you?" The voice, as before, seemed to come from inside the head of the spider rather than from the jaws dangling below.

There was no fear in Olvia this time, seeing the massive creature, rather, she found herself feeling irritated by it. "Yes," she replied. "I can hear you."

It took a few steps forward, towards Olivia, she didn't flinch but was amazed by how silent its movements were. "I saw others at the edge of the camp, I tried to call out to them, but they couldn't hear me. Just like before. But you, you can hear me. I would have called you, but I didn't know your name."

"My name is Olivia," she said quickly. "And where were you?"

The spider didn't respond. In fact, it remained perfectly still. Olivia realized how hard communication would be with this creature. His expression did not change. A spider's body consists of a hard, hair-covered exoskeleton. There are no facial muscles or features that change with mood or attitude. She had once read in a book that seventy percent of human communication is nonverbal. Body language, facial expressions, and even the way you are standing or sitting communicates so much important information. That means, with this spider, she was only receiving thirty percent that someone would normally derive from a conversion with a human. Olivia felt her irritation with the creature boil.

"Where were you? We needed you! Someone died yesterday, and if you had been there to help us, they may be alive." Never in a million years did Olivia think she would be scolding a spider. Especially one that was large enough to look Olivia straight in the eyes. The spider took a step back, its body tucking ever so slightly behind its front legs. Perhaps this was spider body language for shock or shame, Olivia couldn't tell for sure. But at least she was dealing with more than thirty percent now.

"I was on the roof, hiding from you," the spider's voice finally replied. Olivia shook her head and had to look away from the creature. "I was hungry, and I heard you speaking to someone, though I couldn't understand what they were saying."

"That was Will, I told him about you. He wouldn't have hurt you. Besides, you came here tonight, being hungry isn't a problem now."

"I ate extra tonight. Notice there are none of the things in the dark."

Olivia paused for a moment. That was true, this evening they hadn't seen any of the things they called nightcrawlers. It would seem that the theory was correct, and that this spider was eating them. "What do you know about those things?"

"I know that they are not like normal people, they have no fear of being hurt, and they are filled with death and darkness, not life like others. They vibrate differently than everything else. Everything vibrates to me now, all living things, plants, and animals. But they feel like dirty and murky water, sloshing back and forth without life. Beyond that, I know nothing."

"You said that you couldn't understand Will, what did he sound like?"

"It sounds like another language, jumbled up and impossible to understand."

"But you understand me?"

"Yes, perfectly."

"Fine, if you can understand me, then tell me why you didn't help us."

The creature stayed silent for a moment, then moved its head as if it were looking away. "I was afraid. I was hungry and didn't want to hurt the man you were with." It turned its head back to face her. "I am sorry your friend died."

Olivia felt some of her anger and frustration dissipate. She couldn't blame the creature for being afraid. She thought of how hard it would be to be in its position, unable to communicate. She also considered Sheila, and how she had been unforgiving of Olivia, Will, and everyone in the camp. Olivia didn't want to be angry and hateful. She let out a quick breath. "It's ok."

The spider seemed to relax, untucking itself from behind its legs. "But," she continued. "In the future, we really could use your help. Will already knows about you, and I told him that we can trust you."

"Why did you say that?" the creature asked.

"Because that's what I feel, and if it weren't true, I think you would have killed me."

The spider remained motionless for a moment, "I won't hurt you, or anyone."

Olivia nodded. "You said you were looking for me. What did you want to say?"

"I wanted to tell you that the camp with the bad people in it is on the move, they are searching. The woods have been filled with them. I suspect they are looking for you and your people. They are angry, more angry than normal. You are not safe here."

"We're going to move camp tomorrow, across the river to a safe place by the giant tree."

"Good, I will follow and try to keep you safe. I will also keep the things that move at night away from you all when the night comes."

"Thank you," Olivia replied. She paused for a moment, then asked: "You said that the things in the night have vibrations, and it's different than us."

"Yes," the spider replied. "I can feel these vibrations in my hairs."

"What do the bad people in the other camp feel like?"

"Like a pot of overflowing, boiling water."

Olivia thought about this response for a moment. The description of the Rabid didn't surprise her at all, what intrigued her was the phrase that it had used. A pot of boiling water. That was a very human expression. "I told you, my name. Now, you tell me yours." The spider was silent, and unmoving again. "You were human once, weren't you?"

The spider remained still for several moments, then slowly and silently drew back into the darkness out of view. "Not a good one," it said before disappearing entirely.

3

Surprisingly, Olivia was able to get a good sleep that night. She decided to sleep outside next to the tent, fearful that she would wake the resting families inside. The evening had been relatively warm, and her flannel was all she had needed. Perhaps the exhaustion of not only the events of the previous day, but also the little sleep she had gotten when the nightcrawlers had appeared had allowed her to rest deeply. Waking up to the gradual increase of the sunrise had also been a soft and wonderful way for Oliva to be welcomed to the new day.

She took some time to lay where she was with her eyes shut, waiting for the camp to awaken before she was willing to surrender this small spot of peace that she had found. It wasn't long before she became aware of people moving around and starting their day. She kept her eyes closed for some time, but when she heard Will and Dr. Travis's voices, she decided to abandon her sanctuary of rest.

Stirring up, and following the sound of the voices, Olivia found Will and Dr. Travis standing at the edge of the camp, in the spot where Sheila's tent should have been.

"Looks like Sheila left sometime in the night, or very early this morning," Will said, seeing Olivia walking up to the two of them. "Packed up her tent and took everything with her."

Olivia shook her head. For a moment the three of them stood in silence.

'Should we go after her," Olivia finally asked.

"I don't know if it's a good idea," Will replied. "We need to move camp today, and we need to find more food for the people. Given that we ate the last of what we had last night. Not to mention we have no idea how much of a head start she has on us."

"I say good riddance," Dr. Travis said firmly. "She wants to leave, let her leave. Even if we did find her there's no guarantee that she would even come back with us. We certainly aren't going to keep her captive in the camp. Besides, she made it pretty clear how she felt about all of us last night."

"She was hurt and angry when she said those things," Olivia retorted, but was careful to keep her tone calm. "But you're certainly not wrong about everything else. It's not like we can force her to be here."

Will unshouldered his hunting rifle. "If everyone is going to move today, which we need to do, given the lack of supplies that are needed for everyone, we will need to eat before we make that trip." He turned away and started to head for the woods, leaving Olivia and Dr.

Travis behind. Olivia quickly followed him, now gripped by a sense of urgency.

"Will, wait up," she called, her voice was hushed, and Will picked up on the tone.

"What is it?"

"I think we need to move camp as soon as possible."

"Why? These people need to eat, and they may not be ready to move."

Olivia explained to Will about how the spider appeared to her last night and what it had said about the rabid camp being on the hunt for them. She was sure to tell him about the spider's promise to guard the camp from afar but did leave out the details of her crying in the woods.

Will let out a deep sigh, "Ok, perhaps we can find some food while we are on the way to the tree. I will say, it is good to know that he's willing to help us out. Whoever he is."

"I think he was a person, you know, a regular human before the Sphere came." Olivia omitted the part where he stated that he wasn't a good one.

"Well, stranger things have happened."

Olivia laughed, "Yes, in this new, weird world of ours."

Will, Olivia, and Dr. Travis announced to everyone that they would move camp as soon as possible. To Olivia's surprise, few protested, and soon, much of the camp was packing up their belongings. Olivia helped where she could, but much of the work was quickly done, given that there were fewer tents and supplies than there were people now. Many hands make light work, as the expression goes.

With the majority of everything packed up into backpacks, a few duffel bags, and even a wheelbarrow that Olivia had never noticed before, the next thing was to bring as much water with them as possible. Olivia loaned out all the extra bottles and thermoses that she had and gave them to others in the camp who did not have the means to transport water on their own. Unsurprisingly, most of these people were survivors from the cages, who had nothing but dirty clothes on their backs. No one had asked where Sheila was - at least no one asked Olivia - and she found herself rather grateful for this.

With everyone and their belongings assembled, the large group now headed out and left the campsite behind them. Olivia had described the location of her old neighborhood, and Will seemed to know the general area well. The immediate concern was getting the survivors over the bridge, which was blocked by crashed cars at both ends, not to mention the spider's home at its base that would be impossible to conceal from the group. Considering the members of their group, Olivia and Will agreed to not try the bridge. Rather, a little way down the river, away from the bridge, there was a shallow spot in the river that would be much easier to cross. Will had discovered this spot when he was hunting for deer previously and knew that the river was only around a foot deep in this spot. That would bring them to the other side of the river and make a much more direct walk to the neighborhood than going around, taking the bridge, then taking the road that curved around to reach the neighborhood. The only drawback of this plan was that it would most likely be through the forest and other areas that neither Olivia nor Will had seen yet. Still, if the rabid were looking for them, then taking the open road where the large caravan of survivors could be easily spotted would put them in an easy place to be discovered. Besides, Olivia had seen Rick himself on that road only a few days ago, meaning that he was aware of its presence. The journey may be more difficult, but it would be safer, and more likely to yield deer for Will to get.

In a long line of between two or three wide, the group moved down through the forest. They moved like a long snake, with Will and Olivia leading the way, both of whom held their weapons out and ready in case anything with yellow eyes and a nasty attitude decided to show itself. Still, nothing happened. After some time of marching, they eventually came to the spot where the river was shallow, the sound of flowing water grew louder and louder as they approached, and Olivia feared that Will was leading them to some treacherous rapids that couldn't possibly be traversed by their group. However, what they found was a shallow spot in the river, only about a foot deep, that had a bottom of mostly rocks that were small and easy to cross. Stepping through the water, Olivia realized that the bottom consisted of the small rocks that were under the old train tracks that had been there before the Sphere turned the long train path into a flowing river.

Will went across first, with no hesitation, or problems. Olivia followed but decided to remain in the center of the river to offer aid to any who were having a difficult time passing through. As she crossed, she kept her feet low to the bottom, dragging them across the rocky surface below to locate the invisible rails that were surly present under the water. She did this fearing that someone would trip over them and wanted them discovered to warn the ones crossing behind her. To her surprise, she could not find them, it seemed that they had either been buried by the rocky bottom or had disappeared entirely. For a moment, she considered how this could be, but surrendered to the realization that she would probably never know.

The group began passing across the river with little issue, even the older man who had been playing the guitar the night before seemed to stride through the flowing water with ease. Tiffany carried her daughter across the water, and Megan carried hers as well. Dr. Travis held the boy, whose name Olivia had not yet learned, in his arms as they crossed. Then, it was the wheelbarrow's turn to cross, and a team of the men each took a corner of it, hoisted it above their shoulders and crossed the waters as a team. This display seemed to give Megan's children a kick, as they stared and pointed at the team with some kind of childlike wonder and fascination.

Behind them, the end of the group was finally crossing the river, and Olivia noticed that Melody was walking there with them. It took a moment for Olivia to realize exactly who she was looking at. The bags that were under Melody's eyes the night before had only gotten worse, if Olivia had not known better, she would have thought that Melody had applied a shade of makeup under them. Her hair seemed to have lost some of its vibrant blond color and faded to an almost gray, yellow color; it appeared stringy and knotted in some places. She even appeared to have lost some weight in the time between this morning and when Olivia had spoken to her just last night, her facial features seemed sunken in, and she had a nearly emaciated look.

Refusing to let this grotesque change continue for another moment, Olivia stepped over to Melody. "Melody, are you alright?" She put her hand on Melody's shoulder in a gesture of compassion, she was surprised how cold she felt, even through the shirt she was wearing.

Melody slowly turned her head to Olivia, her face seemed almost as if it were in some kind of exhausted trance. "I really don't feel good," she finally said weakly.

"Travis," Olivia called back, now putting both of her hands on Melody to stabilize her.

Dr. Travis came sloshing up to them, he was about to say something but stopped before he began at the sight of Melody. "Melody," he asked. "Can you hear me?"

Melody only nodded her head but remained in the same dream-like trance that she had been in. "Let's get her out of the water," Olivia said.

"Yes, can you give us a hand," Dr. Travis asked one of the men wading through the water here at the end. He picked her up and carried her out of the water, bringing her onto the shore where Will was still waiting. The man set Melody on the grass.

"Melody," Dr. Travis continued, looking into her eyes. "Can you tell me what you're feeling?"

"Cold, and tired, I'm hungry."

Olivia pulled the two granola bars that she had saved from the night before out of her pocket and handed them to Dr. Travis. "Would you like to try to eat these?"

Melody weakly nodded her head, and Dr. Travis handed one of the bars to her. She attempted to open the wrapping but did not seem to have the strength or the dexterity to do it. Dr Travis took her hand in his and placed his fingers inside her wrists, counting the pulses that he found there. His face communicated concern. "Are you experiencing any other symptoms," he asked, counting the beats a second time.

Melody didn't answer for an agonizingly long time before finally answering, "I feel like my mind is being pushed out of my head."

Determining that Melody was too weak to continue, the decision was made to take the things out of the wheelbarrow, which were then carried by others, and have Melody ride in it. Blankets and pillows were provided for her not only to make the metal wheelbarrow more comfortable to ride in but also for her warmth. Despite the heat of the day rising, Melody remained cold. Pushing forward, the group resumed its journey, Dr. Travis remained walking next to Melody as she was pushed along with everyone.

Luckily, the terrain was easier on this side of the river, where it gave way to a lower marshland, with small ponds of water that the group maneuvered through. The ground around the water was muddy at the edges, but remained firm and grassy for the most part, allowing the group to traverse with relative ease. Will kept a keen eye out for deer and excitedly pointed out deer tracks in the muddy banks to Olivia when he came across them.

"These are fresh," he whispered, peering at the surrounding area. It wasn't much farther before they came to a clearing in the woods that was home to a large pond, the bright blue sky opened wide above them revealing the Sphere peering down at them. In the distance, looming above the tree line, was the massive tree. The group stopped for a moment, caught off guard by its size.

"Guessing that's the giant tree you were talking about," Will remarked.

"What gave it away?" Olivia teased, causing Will to smile and shake his head. Will suddenly tensed and his eyes focused on the edge of the pond, about fifty feet away. A group of deer were standing at the pond's edge, walking towards the bank.

"Yes," Will said to himself, bringing up his rifle and taking aim at one of the deer. He stood still for a moment, steadying his aim, while Olivia stood next to him with her fingers in her ears waiting for the shot to ring out. It didn't come.

Olivia looked over at Will, who was no longer looking through the rifle scope. He seemed to be peering in confusion at something.

"What is it," Olivia asked.

"Something is moving in the water."

At first glance, Olivia didn't see anything. The large pond that the small herd of deer was standing next to seemed serene and picturesque. Birds chirped, and the sun rays streamed through the trees in the most beautiful fashion. The only real movement that seemed to be happening was the ripples moving across the water of the pond. *There was no wind that could be causing the ripples*, Olivia thought to herself. At first, she could see nothing that could be contributing to this, everything seemed still. The surface of the water directly in front of where the deer were churned briefly, sending out more ripples and causing the deer's heads to stand up, alerted at the sudden movement. For a moment, everything was still and serene.

The water exploded where the deer were standing as a massive oval shape with a triangle protrusion at its front heaved out of the water, the protrusion in front extended out and parted like massive jaws that launched forward and seized one of the deer in its grasp. The animal let out a weak high-pitched moaning sound as it was hoisted high into the air, its comrades scattered at the sudden rush of movement. Olivia could hardly believe what her eyes were beholding. Behind her, many of the members of the group screamed and recoiled at the massive creature making itself known to the world.

The turtle's leathery dark green head held the deer in its massive pincer-like jaws, as a single eye on the side of its head darted around at the surrounding landscape, then settled on the group, of whom some were still audibly reacting to the behemoth. The head was held out of the massive shell by a long neck, thick with muscle and rolls of rough reptilian flesh. Its massive shell was like an island that had risen out of the depths of the pond like some dangerous leviathan, ancient and terrible. The deer, which appeared small now in its cruelly hooked jaws still struggled, suspended high in the air. With little sound or display, the massive turtle slipped back into the pond, dragging its prey down under the water with it. The water rippled for a minute, then returned to the serene and quiet state it had been in previously. As if nothing had happened.

"What was that?" A voice from the group called out.

"A snapping turtle," Will replied, clearly stunned by what he had seen. "They're common in this part of the US, though not normally that big."

"Are we in danger?" Olivia asked.

"Depends, it should stay in the water. What we saw was probably its normal hunting pattern. If I'm not mistaken, they only leave the water to lay eggs. I think we will be safe if we stay far away from that pond."

There was no debate in the group over this course of action. Taking a sharp left turn away from the pond, the group moved towards the edge of the clearing, nearly five hundred feet away from the edge of the pond, and stopped their travel to rest there. It was approaching noon now, and hunger had set itself into the forefront of everyone's mind.

"We can't continue any further until we can feed these people," Will remarked firmly to Olivia and Travis, who with many others in the group agreed intently with this assertion. "We only need one deer; a single deer can feed over two hundred mouths. I can track the ones that the turtle scared away, I'm sure I saw them flee in this direction. I should be able to find their trail soon. I doubt they would have gotten far."

"Good," Dr. Travis commented. "I doubt that Melody can go much further. I would like her to be able to rest and let me assess her condition further."

"I'm willing to bet we're almost halfway to the neighborhood," Olivia remarked. "If we have to stop anywhere, this is probably the best place."

Will was already dropping his pack and the duffel bag his tent was stuffed in. "Be sure everyone is mindful to not drink all of their water."

Will ventured in the direction of the pond, looking down and carefully inspecting the ground as he went. Seeming to find what he was looking for, Olivia watched him kneel low to the ground, then turn sharply away to the left and disappear into the tree line. Two of the men from the group, who had carried the wheelbarrow across the river, followed him into the trees.

The others, who were indeed tired from the trek, and from taking the journey on an empty stomach, unloaded very little in the way of their new camp. Several only dropped their packs and things onto the ground and lay down on the soft grass. Everyone would periodically cast weary glances in the direction of the pond. While others ventured off a small ways to forage for berries, and anything else to eat.

"Was that a sea monster, Mom?" Megan's young boy emphatically asked his mother, a childish wonder in his eyes. Olivia felt herself give a small smile at the innocence of the young boy's question.

4

An audible sound of excitement and relief rose from the camp when Will and the other two returned from their hunt a short time later, a large doe in toe behind them. Tiffany had already begun work on the cooking station when they arrived and positioned the tripod with its metal grated cooking surface dangling over the fire several others had constructed in the center of their temporary, nomadic home. Two cast iron skillets would also serve to prepare the meat for everyone lying directly in the coals of the burning fire.

Hunting the food, skinning and processing the deer had taken time. Now, evening was falling. Making further travel impossible. The decision to make camp for the night was unanimous. There was a second fire burning now - with a few more being lit around the perimeter of the camp to ward off the crawlers - this second fire was positioned next to Melody, who was lying in a sleeping bag, with a blanket over the top of it, a large soft pillow supporting her head. Her condition had only worsened since the river, she was now virtually immobile, only able to mutter weakly. Dr. Travis had attempted to feed her the venison when it was served by Tiffany and Will, but it only yielded vomiting from Melody.

"I don't think it's an infection," Dr. Travis postulated. "There's no fever. So, I don't believe there is a risk of the group becoming affected, besides, as I said before, I haven't seen any infection or disease since the Sphere came. She is having cold sweats, and her lips appear to be turning purple. If I didn't know better, I would say it resembles a heroin overdose. But it's been lasting for too long, almost like it's in slow motion or something. I saw several of them when I was working in Minneapolis, it looks very much like that."

"I don't think it's that," Olivia chimed in. "She has been acting strange for a while now. She's a vegetarian, she made a bit of a scene about it the night before you all came to our camp. Then, last night she ate meat. I tried to ask her about it, and she didn't react. Almost like she didn't know that it was a weird thing for her to do."

"Well, eating meat wouldn't do this," Dr. Travis remarked dismissively.

Olivia considered telling him that the food being the culprit wasn't what she meant but decided to drop it. While Melody's condition was not good, over the course of the evening, it did not seem to get any worse. Still, Olivia found herself bracing for Melody's death to be announced sometime during the night. Olivia decided to sleep outside. The tent that she had been sharing with the two mothers and their kids had become very cramped, and Olivia was unsure if she would be able to sleep in its confinements again. Nina protested when she discovered this, wanting Olivia to sleep in the tent again. After some discussion, Olivia agreed to sleep just outside of the tent entrance, and that only the screen door of the tent would be zipped shut. Olivia considered this to be a good trade.

Before laying down for the evening, Olivia took a short walk to the edge of the camp, where several fires meant to ward off the crawlers burned brightly, casting their rays like a wall of light that the things couldn't cross. There were none of the things in the woods and Olivia wondered if the spider, their unseen ally in the darkness, was silently eliminating the threat. For a moment, she thought she saw his long, hairy legs in the darkness beyond the light's reach, but it was simply the branch of a low-hanging tree. Still, she was grateful for his help.

Morning arrived, and Olivia awoke to the soft rising of the sun. She went to the edge of camp and relieved herself behind a tree. Upon returning, she was greeted with the sound of loud moaning, punctuated with high-pitched shrieks and painful growling. Moving quickly to the source of the sound, which seemed to be inside the camp, Olivia arrived to find Dr. Travis caring for Melody. On the ground, and still in the sleeping bag she had been placed in last night, Melody wailed and shrieked, with long guttural growls that sounded as if they would tear her vocal cords. Dr. Travis, who tried to hold her still, was attempting to calm her.

"What's happening," Olivia demanded.

"I don't know," Dr. Travis shouted, clearly struggling to keep the small girl held down. "I found her this morning with the blanket pulled over her head, I took it off to check on her and she reacted. Help me hold her!"

Olivia flung herself down and tried to hold Melody's arms still but was quickly overcome by the strength the small girl had. "I can't," she exclaimed.

The commotion had drawn the attention of many of the people in the camp, most of whom watched with fear and concern. Will emerged from the group. "What's happening, what can I do?"

"Help us to hold her," Dr. Travis yelled.

Melody let out a long and loud growl again, it sounded strained and visceral as if an animal of some violent nature were inside of her crying out. Mixed in with the horrid sound was something else that Olivia heard. A voice, slimy and deep. "Hold me," he asked in an acidic and incredulous tone, it filled with both hate and amusement. "Nothing? Still you understand nothing!" The voice that sounded from within Melody herself and not a production of her lips, which were snarled and baring teeth. The voice sent shivers down Olivia's spine and caused her to be covered with gooseflesh. Every hair on her neck stood in terrified attention.

"Did you hear that," Olivia asked the others.

"Hear what," Dr. Travis dismissively asked.

"That voice, I heard it coming from her, did you hear it?"

"What, what voice," Will asked, his voice strained from the struggle with Melody.

"You, you hear my words," The voice demanded of Olivia. Melody stopped struggling and turned her head to face Olivia, her eyes appeared to be a gray color, and her lips still did not move in sync with the voice yet growled as they had before. "How, how do you understand?"

"Who are you?" Olivia asked the voice.

"What are you doing," Dr. Travis demanded of Olivia.

"Is something speaking, Olivia?" Will asked, seemingly grasping that Olivia had begun a conversion that they were not privy to.

"Only you can hear me," The voice said, the hateful amusement back to his voice. "You will be a problem for me. No matter. One day, I will remove you. Or, perhaps, now."

A well of confidence filled Olivia. She didn't want Melody to suffer under whatever this thing was. "Get out, get out of her now!"

A hideous laughter sounded from within Melody. Deep with cruelty, mocking, and hatefulness. Again, it mingled with Melody's laughter. "Very well."

A cold wind began to pick up around them, starting low and calm but growing to a howl. The very air itself seemed to become heavy, Olivia became aware that her breath was becoming visible before her eyes. The wind continued to pick up, and many of the people who were standing around began to draw back glancing around in confusion and fear. Melody's mouth fell open, and a black inky mist began to leak out of her mouth and her nostrils, it swirled up into the air and gathered in a growing pillar of complete blackness. As though thick black oil had been spilled in the air and was swirling up of its own accord. The wind intensified as the looming black shape took form high above them, Olivia and the others fell back and scrambled away from the gathering darkness. It grew taller and taller into the air, towering over the camp by at least twenty feet.

It bellowed and swirled, and darkness seemed to seep from its inky form. Despite the rising sun in the distance, the darkness emitting from the thing seemed to swallow up the light around it. As if it brought the very night itself and was spreading it out like a foul stench in the air. The form then took shape at its uppermost parts, and Olivia found herself facing a pair of eyes glaring out from inside the swirling darkness. Long arms appeared, capped with dangerous clawed hands. Even with these familiar shapes forming from the grotesque black shapes, they continued to shift and swirl, as if they had no true form of their own. It moved and flowed like black ooze being poured into a vessel of water. Their eyes fixed on Olivia.

"Who am I, you ask?" The voice dripped with malice and filled the air all around everyone. "You ask me such a question, from your place of ignorance. Do you not recognize, do you not know? Do you not recall who ruled you, who ruled all of you?" His long smokey arm flung out in a gesture of accusation and dominance to the camp around him. "I am still your god, as I was before. I ruled this world, and I will rule it again. Nothing has changed, that cursed thing in the sky cannot take that from me. No, nothing has changed. Nothing! I was here in the beginning. He who created has no authority. Nothing is new! All that has happened now is the things that were hidden have been made apparent to all. Can you not see? Even you worthless underlings who cannot recognize your master. You will worship me again, as your leaders did before. You worshiped me with your anger and your lust, your complacency, and your greed, they will all bow down to me again. And you ask who am I? I am your god. I am god, god of the world before and soon, this world too. I will have it back, regardless of how weak it has made me, weakness is temporary! The world will submit to me again, nothing will stop that. Not the creator, not his pet, not you. I will rule this world again. Starting with all of you, you will all be mine! Your will is irrelevant. You are all mine; this world is mine!"

Olivia was looking up in horror at the being, its height grew and grew as it spoke, its voice booming across the land, its darkness overcoming the sun above, the cold air piercing her skin. She gripped tightly to the grass, unable to move or stand. Tears streamed down her face. Fear and hopelessness filled her soul and she found herself unable to speak. In the deepest recesses of her mind, Olivia feared that she would never feel happiness again, never feel joy, never feel love. All she could do was grip tightly to the grass beneath her.

A scratching feeling in her palms pulled Olivia's attention away from the dread and torment in her mind, she looked down and saw long grass pushing through between her fingers. She wiped the tears out of her eyes and took another glance. The grass was indeed sprouting, growing longer with small yellow and white flowers sprouting from their tips. She looked around and saw the others in her company lying in the grass as she was, they too seemed to have been crying with their eyes red and tears on their faces, the grass was sprouting around them as well.

Small orbs of light floated in the air around her, and the air turned warm. Olivia's breath was becoming invisible again. Replacing the piercing cold was a feeling of electricity in the air as if the very breath of the atmosphere was singing silently. The darkness that was emanating from the black smokey shape seemed to retreat into the monster, replaced by a warm blue sky and dancing orbs of light. The dreadful fear and torture of her spirit began to slip away, being overcome by hope.

A loud and powerful snort sounded behind Olivia, she turned her head away from the towering blackness and saw two massive hooved feet standing like strong trees. She cast her gaze upwards and found herself looking up to see the giant buck that she had seen a few days ago. It stood strong and proud, its chest was out, and its head was held up high. Eyes firmly and intently fixed upon the being of darkness.

"You," the voice from the darkness shrieked, its mocking tone was completely gone now and only the hateful venom remained. "They're mine, mine!" The thing let out a bone-chilling shriek. And extended its long arms out wide, the darkness emitting from it pressed out and Olivia felt the fear and hopelessness return to her.

The buck let out another snort and stomped one of its massive hooves hard to the ground, it lowered its head down and pointed its massive antlers at the monster, a posture of intimidation. With its eyes firmly fixed still, it let out another snort and stomped its hoof again. The orbs of light intensified and the tingle of the air around it hummed audibly. The darkness again retreated, being pushed back it quickly dissipated and dissolved into the monster, who seemed to shrink with a hateful hiss.

The hideous creature held up its arms in a defensive posture. Its glowing red eyes burned with a fiery intensity. With a horrifying screech that caused everyone to cover their ears, the thing lifted into the air and whisked away, streaming itself through the air like an aerial serpent, disappearing over the open meadow and into the forest.

The light of the morning returned, and the feeling of fear and dread left everyone. The massive deer stood back up, chest out, head held high and proud. It slowly turned and returned to the woods, the floating orbs of light, the magic in the air, and the sprouting grass following with it.

5

It took the group several minutes to recover from the experience. Everyone was on the ground, lying amongst the grass that was now longer than it had been before, its long green tips had pushed their way through the camping equipment and the other objects that had been laid on the ground. Somewhere amongst the grass, Olivia could hear a moaning sound, as if someone were lying in the grass struggling with unbearable pain. "Will," she called out. "Will!"

"I'm ok," Wills's voice called back. "Is everyone ok?"

Various voices called out that they were ok, or that they thought so. Olivia was able to hear Tiffany's voice amongst the voices.

Dr. Travis cursed out suddenly, "Will, Olivia, get over here!"

Olivia was able to stand, now able to see above the long grass, which was around a foot and a half high. Dr. Travis was standing over the cot where Melody was lying, which also seemed to be the source of the moaning sound. Olivia ran over to them, joining Will about halfway to where they were.

Melody was still lying on the cot; the blanket and the sleeping bag were in haphazard disarray around her. She moaned lightly; her arms were held up lazily shielding her face from the morning light. Her eyes seemed hazed and though they wandered around, they did not focus on anything. There was something almost trance-like in her stare, her skin was ashen gray, and Olivia recognized the look of her immediately. "Nightcrawler," she said out loud.

Six

Truth

1

"Ok, so we need to kill her then," Dr. Travis asserted to the group.

"We can't just kill her, Travis," Will replied firmly.

"Then what are we going to do?"

"We're not going to kill Melody," Olivia said, her voice also firm and determined.

"Well, since you all know everything, then, what is the cure for this situation?" Dr. Travis snapped back. He had taken several steps back from the cot that Melody, or what had been Melody, lay on.

"I don't know, Travis. But we are not killing her," Will's words were slow and deliberate.

"Can we leave her here?" Tiffany asked. Nina stood behind her, clutching her mother's leg.

"What good will that do? You said they came out at night, she will just follow us when the sun sets, and then we will have to worry about her snatching someone up. Could be your little girl if you're not careful," Dr. Travis said in a taunting voice.

Will stepped in between Dr. Travis and the others, Melody, and Tiffany both stood behind his back. "Walk away, now." Olivia stepped over next to Will.

Mr. Gregovski, the old man who had been playing the guitar, walked over to Melody and laid the blanket back over the top of her head. Beneath the blanket, Melody stopped moving and remained motionless, ceasing her moaning. Mr. Gregovski then waved his hand over the blanket. This gesture produced no reaction, he then poked where her face was under the blanket. Again, no reaction. Mr. Gregovski looked up at Dr. Travis.

Dr. Travis glanced around at everyone; it was obvious that he was alone in this matter. "Fine, but she needs to be tied up too." He looked around at everyone watching. "Look, I'm not trying to be the bad guy here, I just don't want this thing hurting any of us."

"We know, Travis," Olivia replied, she kept her voice calm and compassionate. She didn't want another person leaving the camp like Sheila had. "What else can we do to make sure everyone is safe?"

He looked at the blanket, then let out a long sigh, "I don't know, just keep her tied up."

"We can do that," Will said.

"Ok, sorry."

"It's ok, she's a part of our group. We're not giving up on her yet."

"What was that thing that came out of her," Tiffany asked.

"I've never seen that thing," Olivia said. "But I have seen that deer." Olivia took a moment to explain her encounter the other day when it crossed the road.

"So, you saw it before on this side of the river." Will considered Olivia's comment. "Hm… that's good if we settle over here," Will commented.

"How?" Tiffany asked.

"Because that big thing that came out of the girl was chased away by it," Mr. Gregovski stated. "It would be nice if that big buck was in our backyard, keeping him away."

Tiffany gave Olivia a questioning glance. "You were talking to it before it came out of her, you told it to come out. How did you do that?"

Will cast Olivia a cautious look.

"I don't know, I heard it speaking in her voice. I didn't know it would listen to me. Everyone could hear it after it came out?"

The group acknowledged that they did. "Something about it being a god, and we will worship it," Dr. Travis commented. "What was that about?"

"I think it meant what it said," Mr. Gregovski postulated. "It was some kind of spirit, or something. It used to run this world, or at least tried to. I've been around long enough to know that evil is a real thing. Sounds like, whatever it is, it's fixing to take this world back."

"Good reason to stay on this side of the river, close to that big buck," Will said as he knelt next to the covered form of Melody, who remained motionless beneath the blanket. "Wonder if that's how they're made." He staired at the blanketed teen.

"What do you mean?" Olivia asked, following his gaze.

"Well, that thing was in her, but I don't think it always was. She started acting differently a day ago. I wonder if it gets inside of them. Changes them, or maybe takes something from them. Drains them of life till it's done. Then leaves a crawler behind."

"She was getting weaker and weaker. Suppose that makes sense," Mr. Gregofski said.

"Now, let's not get too carried away here," Dr. Travis interjected. "We don't know any of that. This is all speculation. Besides, we should also be considering the fact that whatever that thing was, it made a big show. I'm sure its screeching was heard for some distance. I'd hate to be sitting here when our old, yellow-eyed friends show up."

"He's right," Will said. "We should get moving. Our plan is the same. We get to the tree. Hopefully, it's safer where Olivia was describing."

"Hope that big buck keeps that thing away too," Mr. Gregofski said, standing back up. "We are still going to take the girl, right?"

"Yes," Will said, looking at Dr. Travis.

"As long as she stays tied up," he replied.

2

The group made it to the hedge wall without any interference, though there was some difficulty navigating through the vegetation that had grown thick in this area. They pushed through the small hole in the brush wall that Olivia had used a few days ago, it was still concealed, but Olivia located it quickly with the piece of cloth she had tied a few days prior. For the most part, the passing through had been easy, that is, until they had to drag Melody through the passage. She had been bound by her wrists and ankles, a task that she didn't resist, as long as her face was covered. She was then transferred back into the wheelbarrow and carted here easily enough. However, the wheelbarrow had to be set on its wheel and its back legs to fit through the passage, then dragged by Will in the front, and pushed by one of the men in the back.

Now, with everyone behind the hedge wall, all twenty-two of their company - including Melody - everyone felt a sense of safety. Everyone also stood in awe of the tree. It remained the same as when Oliva had last seen it, towering high above the landscape. The Sphere watched from above.

Will shook his head looking up at it. "So, you planted this?"

"It was smaller then," Olivia teased. This earned a smile from Will.

"Let's check the wall, make sure it really does circle around the whole place. We should look for holes like this one."

Will, and the group spread out, one group traversed the length of the wall in one direction, and the other took the other direction. Will took one group and Olivia traveled with one of the men from the group and Mr. Gregofski.

"Don't you want to rest, Mr. Gregofski?" Olivia asked.

"Young lady, my knees and body feel better than they have in 30 years. I may be gray, but I'm kicking. And, please, call me Lew. Short for Lewis."

Olivia smiled at the charming old man. "Ok, Lew, you have it your way."

"I'm Tim, by the way," the younger man said. Holding out his hand and shaking Olivia's. "I never got to thank you for saving us from that cage."

They continued around, following the wall, it stretched on for a good way. Forming an oval shape around the base of the tree, Olivia kept her shotgun at her hip in case anything troublesome decided to present itself. Nothing did. Eventually, they connected with Will and his group at the far end of the wall.

"Anything?" he asked.

"Nothing, it's solid the whole way around. Can't even see through it."

"That's good," Will said. "We found a patch where it is a little lower than the rest, and thinner, still over our heads by a foot or two, but other than that it's solid the whole way around."

Olivia thought about this for a moment. How did Sue get out then, did she come across the passage and crawl out too? And did Rick do the same? Why? It seemed strange to her. And, for that matter, did Adam crawl out too? Did he encounter them? Did they kill him? Olivia pushed the thoughts from her mind. Now wasn't the time.

The group reconvened outside of Olivia's house, she entered the home with Will, and the two of them emptied all the canned food from the house cupboards that had been left. Will saw the garage and how Olivia had set it up a few days before.

"This place is still good; I'd stay here if I were you."

"I was going to invite Tiffany, Megan, and the kids to stay here. My bedroom is still intact."

"The roof caved in in your living room. I'd be worried about mold forming when it rains. Eventually, we're going to have to build permanent shelters."

Olivia opened the cooler she had moved all the food in. The ice had melted, but it was still cool inside. "We will have to figure out food too."

"I think Mr. Gregofski was a farmer or had some kind of garden or something, he mentioned growing carrots, potatoes, onions, and other stuff when we were cooking the other night."

They took their finds outside and rejoined the larger group. They had also taken the time to scavenge through the homes in the neighborhood. A large assortment of items had been found, and the group excitedly discussed the findings. Food, clothing, blankets and pillows, tools in garages, and even camping equipment that could be utilized immediately. But, of all the things they found, many firearms had been discovered in one of the homes. A few rifles, three shotguns, and two pistols were found in one house alone. Accompanied by plenty of ammunition. In total, their group now possessed eleven firearms of varying kinds and sizes.

Everyone had a sense of hope renewed in their spirits. The safety of the wall, and the abundance of food, supplies, and arms to protect themselves with. The encouragement was almost enough to push the memory the monster that came out of Melody to the back of their thoughts. With the exception of Melody herself, who remained motionless beneath her coverings, there seemed to be no sense of danger at all.

Lunch was on many people's minds, since they had skipped breakfast to allow for the travel here. A fire was assembled, and food was prepared. Today's meal was a smorgasbord of assorted canned foods, vegetables, venison from the hunt, and even some chips and candy.

It wasn't long before Lew began to fiddle on the guitar again, playing a song that many in the group began to sing along with. Olivia didn't recognize the tune, but she assumed it was an older song, as even Will was singing along with it. But it didn't matter that she didn't know it, she felt joy watching everyone singing and laughing together. Tiffany sang along, holding Nina on her lap and clapping the little girl's hands together to the beat of the song. Tiffany had a wonderful smile on her face as she sang, as did little Nina. She wondered how long it had been since they smiled like this together.

After the meal, the group began setting up tents, also utilizing the new tents that had been found. Others went looking in the homes, but the damaged buildings offered little shelter. Tim, who used to work construction, was very concerned about the structural strength of the homes, and strongly advised everyone not to sleep in them – until they could do a thorough inspection. Olivia showed Tim the garage, and Tim agreed it was probably OK, but he insisted she not sleep in her room though. Ultimately, the creation of stable housing would be necessary. That is, if the location proved to be safe. Tim felt confident that he could build the shelters they would need.

Their little community was coming together, and Olivia couldn't help but feel hopeful about it. However, their immediate attention fell on Melody. Olivia, together with Will, Dr. Travis, Lew, Tim, and Tiffany discussed what should be done. They decided that she should be put into a small shed that sat on the side of one of the homes. The shed was strong, intact, and had very small windows that even a small girl like Melody couldn't crawl out of. In addition to this, a fire would be kept near the front of the door at night, so that the light would keep her in.

Dr. Travis begrudgingly agreed to the arrangement, but the others could see he wasn't comfortable with it.

3

Evening came, and though the group was indeed in good spirits, wary glances began to be cast at the shed. It was decided to light the fire early, and smaller fires were put around the camp as well. The shed sat at the edge of this ring of fire, so even if Melody did get out, they should be safe as they were nights before. Olivia's mind dwelt on the spider. He said he would be out there, and she was hoping to get some kind of report from him about what was happening around.

As the darkness descended, Olivia found herself pondering the thing that had come out of Melody. Was it lurking in the darkness? If it was, how would they see it? True, they had more weapons now, but there was no way that that could hurt it. It was like a shadow. *How do you hurt a shadow?* Olivia feared seeing growing red eyes in the dark, maliciously fixed on the camp with the desire for domination and enslavement. Hopefully, the large buck was somewhere, keeping it at bay.

Olivia considered the interaction between the shadow monster and the deer. There had been a moment where it had seemed the shadow monster had recognized the deer. She wondered what history they had.

Olivia had directed Megan and Tiffany to sleep in the garage with the kids. She hacked the foliage away from the outside door and pushed the shelf away, allowing them to pass inside without needing to venture through the dilapidated home. Nina, again, implored her to sleep with them. Olivia assured her that she would be sleeping in the tent outside in the front yard. This was partially because she wanted to sleep somewhere where she would be able to get some sleep. She was also desperate for the spider's report. An eight-legged scout, that only she can talk to. What a weird world it was.

Olivia sat down next to the fire that cast its protective rays on the shed, she faced it with a growing sadness in her heart. The shed was mostly silent, though there were a few thumping sounds from time to time inside. The door on the front was latched, but no padlock could be found. A screwdriver from her home was shoved in the hole where a much sturdier lock should be.

The spider, now Melody the nightcrawler. She so desperately wanted to help them both. But how? She could feel it, feel it in her soul that she could help them. But how to accomplish that goal felt impossible to her. There was also the matter of Adam. Would she be able to find her brother? Would she be able to help these people? Or was she setting herself up for failure?

"Taking the first watch?" Will's voice called behind her.

"Yes, though I'm not sure what good it would do."

"Why do you say that?" Will asked as he sat next to her.

"I don't know what I would do if she got out. I understand that the light will hold her back, but still… If she did get out somehow and was a threat, I wouldn't be able to shoot her."

"You're a good person, Liv."

Olivia smiled for a moment. "That's what my brother calls me. Liv."

"We can go look for him now, we have this place now, it seems like we're pretty safe here. I'll still help you if you want."

"I know, and I thank you for that. It's just hard, not knowing if I will find him."

"I think you'll drive yourself crazy if you don't try."

"Yeah, I know." Olivia took a swig of water, noticing her bottle was nearly empty. "We're going to need water soon."

"That will have to be the first thing tomorrow."

"Just so you know, I'm expecting the spider to show up."

"Oh?" Will adjusted uncomfortably. "Should I not be here for that?"

"You can, just remember you probably won't hear him, and he won't be able to understand you."

Will paused for a moment, seemingly looking for the words to say. "Liv, that thing that came out of Melody. You were able to talk to it before it came out."

Olivia was uncomfortable with this, but she knew that the conversation was going to happen. Perhaps, even should happen. "I don't know how. I could just hear it.

Like I do with the spider. I don't try to speak to these things. I just hear them. And, apparently, they hear me. I can't explain it, Will."

"That's ok, and I wasn't asking you to explain it to me. I was wondering though; it seems that there are some of us who are able to do things. Things that others can't do. Talk to things that others can't talk to, like you can. Not die, like I can. My point is; what if there are others out there, or even others in our group who can do special things too?"

"Superpowers, you mean."

"Perhaps, but more than that. We both agree that the Sphere has a plan for us. That it wants us to help it make this world a better place, that we have a job to do here. What if it has given us these gifts so that we can do that job better? When a soldier goes off to war, they are given the tools that they need to do their job. What if these are our tools?"

"I'm not sure how talking to an evil spirit, and a giant spider will help the world-"

"Liv," Will interrupted. His voice suddenly became very serious.

"What?"

"Your friend is here."

Olivia looked around, at first glance, not seeing anything. "Where-"

"The shed."

Olivia looked at the shed, perched on top of it, mostly in the dark, was the spider. Olivia marveled once again at how silent it was. She wondered if it could have been following them the entire time. Remaining silent and unseen just beyond their vision.

"There's a dark one in here," the spider called out.

"Yes, it's our friend. Her name is Melody, we want to help her."

"How will you do that?" the creature asked.

"We don't know yet, but she's our friend. We have to try."

"Wait, are you speaking to it now? Is it speaking? I can't hear anything," Will asked.

"What did the man say," the Spider asked.

"He asked if I'm talking to you now," Olivia replied.

"He can't tell who you're talking to?" Will asked.

"No, I mean yes, I was talking to him," Olivia said.

"I don't understand, do you mean him, or me," the spider asked.

"Both of you, stop talking! Now!" Olivia said firmly, her voice a hair away from a shout.

Will and the Spider fell silent, Olivia looked back towards where the rest of the group was by the tents and central campfire. The others in camp were too engrossed in their own activities. She turned back to them, "Will, he cannot understand what you are saying. Spider, he cannot hear your voice when you speak. I can hear both of you. So, we need to be patient with one another when we speak."

The spider lifted and held one of its front legs up in the air, "I can do this to show I am speaking."

"Yes, that's great," Olivia said.

"Is he asking a question?" Will asked.

Olivia took a breath and let out a frustrated laugh. It was somewhat comical. The giant spider, normally a terrifying creature for anyone to encounter, seemed silly with its leg in the air. It reminded Olivia of a small child urgently trying to ask a teacher a question in a classroom. She pushed hard against the urge to laugh. "If his leg is in the air, he is speaking." Calmly, she turned to the spider, who, thankfully, had returned his leg to gripping the top of the shed. "Spider," she said calmly. "Can you tell us what you have seen on this side of the river?"

The spider returned his leg to the air. "I have seen nothing dangerous on this side of the river. That is strange. Normally, at night, they are out hunting. But, here, near your camp, there are none. Except the one inside this building. There were some next to the river, but they didn't seem interested coming this way."

Olivia turned to Will and translated what was said to him. "Where do they go during the day," Will asked and Olivia repeated.

"They hid in buildings, in thick brush, or even buried themselves in dirt. Two came into my home before Olivia to escape the light." Olivia remembered the two bodies on the floor of the spider's house when she first met him.

"What about the yellow-eyed people," Olivia asked after translating for Will. "Have you seen them?"

"Yes, they were spread out in the woods, searching urgently. But all of them suddenly turned north for some reason, and then went back to their camp. I do not know why."

Olivia told Will what was said, this puzzled him. "Ask him about the thing that came out of Melody," Will said in reply. Olivia described to the spider what they had seen come out of Melody and told him about their theory of how nightcrawlers are made.

"I have never seen something like that, I haven't seen a huge deer either. But I will say this. That thing will never be my god." Olivia told him that they all felt the same way. "If there is nothing else, and I can't eat the one in here, then I must go. My hunger is great."

As the spider silently slipped away, Olivia felt a ping of regret in her heart. If their theory of the crawlers was true, then that would mean each one the spider ate was a person like Melody. She wished so badly that she could help them. Come to think of it, she wasn't even sure if she had tried to talk to one of them. It was her "gift" as Will referred to it. Had she tried to use it on one of them?

"Well," Will remarked, interrupting her thoughts. "Good to know we seem to be safe for now."

"Yes, that's true."

"You go get some sleep, I'll stay here and wait for whoever is on guard next."

Olivia nodded, and she headed to her tent.

4

The next morning was cooler than the day before, and Olivia and Will were grateful for it. Walking down the road that lead to the bridge, and therefore to water would have been even more laborious if it had been done under the heat. A few of the other men from the group had accompanied them, while others had remained back. Tim had deduced that a well could be made in the center of the camp, though time would be needed to finish this project, and they needed water now. Olivia didn't understand how the two bent pieces of metal wire that Tim was using would show where water was underground, but it wasn't something she knew anything about anyway. Will agreed with Tim, and after that commented about how a "dug well" would be perfect for the center of town.

Some were already referring to their new home as "The Town," even if it had been theirs for only one night. In Olivia's mind, it would always be her neighborhood, but she supposed that town worked. It did give the impression of community to the people of their group. It also, and perhaps more importantly, gave the impression of a future. The idea of a future, a sustainable future, was something that everyone wanted to cling to. Tim was probably the most excited of everyone to move forward with this idea, even talking about building different permanent structures for everyone. Others had also excitedly suggested things they would like to see built.

The road, though broken and overgrown, made the wheelbarrow much easier to push along the path than it had been in the overgrown wild they traveled the day before. There was also, amongst the members of this expedition, a feeling of uncertainty about the area that they had traveled on yesterday. The area where they encountered not only the massive shadow monster that emerged from Melody, but also where the giant snapping turtle lived in the pond.

So, they had decided to travel on the road instead. Olivia and Will were both comfortable with this decision, especially after the spider reported about the rabid having retreated to their camp, and the mention of crawlers being scarce in the area around the tree. The crawlers would, of course, be hiding from the light of day, so they did not expect to encounter any of them. Still, Olivia, Will, and one of the men who came with them were all armed.

The landscape hasn't changed since Olivia first saw it only three days ago. It was hard for Olivia to believe that only three days had passed since the Sphere had done its work on the world. So much had changed in that time, not just physically with the world and the forest and the new creatures and people in it, but within Olivia. She had found courage and strength in herself that she wasn't entirely sure was there before. Sure, her father had taught her much about hunting and hiking in the woods, and that helped her greatly during this time. But more surprising to her, she had found the courage to help the people around her. To stand up and face the things that were terrifying and dangerous because it was the right thing to do. She had left her house wanting to find her brother - a task that she still planned to do - and now, she was going on an expedition for water to serve a group of people she had only known for a few days. A group of people she was willing to put herself in harm's way for them.

Had the Sphere changed her? Had it given her a purpose that she was subconsciously fulfilling? Had it turned a first-semester college girl into a leader for these people without her even knowing? The way it took Will, an almost ninety-year-old alcoholic man, and turned him into an immortal defender of his people? Olivia found herself looking up at the Sphere with this thought, she felt that, if the Sphere did indeed change her, who she was down in her core, she was grateful for this person. Perhaps others would become offended by this notion of being transformed into someone new, being made a new creation, Olivia, however, was grateful. She enjoyed the person she had become.

"Let's check out that house over there," one of the men helping with the wheelbarrow called out. Mitch was the man's name; Olivia had learned it before they left that morning. The house that he was referring to was one of the only ones along the way that wasn't completely caved in as the others along the route were. The house had heavy foliage and vegetation growing over it, even over its entrance. A small hole in the roof, where a section of the corner seemed to have caved in, appeared to be the only way inside. Mitch, utilizing an area of raised ground, climbed up the roof of a low porch to get access to the hole.

"Be careful," Olivia called out to him.

"No worries, I've got this," he replied, holding up one of the pistols that they had discovered yesterday. Mitch crawled into the hole, half a moment later, a loud combination of cursing came out of the hole, and Mitch stumbled out of the hole backward. Falling onto his back on the low porch and dropping the gun next to him. Olivia braced herself for the gun to discharge, yet a shot never rang out from it.

"What was it?" Will called out, hurrying over to the house.

"A bunch of those gray-skinned things are in there," Mitch answered breathlessly.

By this time, Olivia and Will had come up to the house, and, upon hearing this, Olivia climbed up to where Mitch was.

"Liv, what are you doing?" Will reacted.

"I need to know if I can talk to them too." She finished her climb and stuck her head inside the large opening. Inside, there was a small landing where the second story of the home had been, and it too was caved in. Below, standing in the darkness, silently looking up and Olivia, were five crawlers. They didn't react or make any sort of sound. Just stared up at her with the same blank, trance-like stare that they always seemed to have. Olivia let out an audible gasp as she discovered that she recognized one of the faces.

"What?" Will asked, reacting to her gasp. His climb up suddenly quicker.

"I know him, he was one of my neighbors in the neighborhood." Olivia pointed to a man, standing in the back of the group of five. It was Greg, the know-it-all guy from the day the Sphere changed everything. He still wore the same clothing as he had that day, only the shirt that he had been wearing was torn at the neck, exposing his chest. She looked around at the other faces, peering up from the darkness below, she didn't recognize any. For this, she was grateful. Finding Adam's face among ones like this was a deep fear she hoped not to confront.

"Hello," Olivia called to them, tentatively. There was no reply or reaction. "Greg, can you understand me?" The thing that had once been her neighbor, who had considered an alien invasion was going to follow the Sphere taking away the electricity of the world, stared back up at her blankly. Nothing about his demeanor indicated that he could understand her. She let out a breath. Part of her was relieved at this, but also part of her was frustrated. She was no closer to understanding this ability that she had of talking to things that others couldn't. She had wondered if she wasn't some kind of translator who could speak to anything in this new world. It seemed she was wrong about that.

The group decided to leave the crawlers there. Mitch had asked if he should kill them, so they wouldn't have to worry about them coming around later. Will decided that they didn't want to fire a gun off unless necessary. Fearing the sound would draw the attention of unwanted guests.

It wasn't long before they arrived at the river. They settled in right at the base of the bridge, the forest now surrounded them again here. They pulled up the wheelbarrow and began filling up all the containers they had brought with them. Olivia took a moment to rinse her face in the river's cold water, then cup her hands and drink. She then filled her water bottle.

Will crouched next to her, "So, they didn't respond to you talking to them?"

"No, I didn't hear anything."

"Honestly, I'm not surprised."

"What do you mean?"

Will took a moment to gather his thoughts before speaking. "I don't think they are conscious. Like their souls are gone, there's a word for it. A thing that has a soul."

"Sentient?"

"Sure, that sounds right. Remember when Melody said that she felt like her mind was being pushed out of her head? When I look at those things, it doesn't seem like they are there. Like their souls have been taken away or pushed out. I think that's why you can't talk to them, there's nothing inside for you to talk to."

Olivia considered this for a moment. "Then what does that mean for Melody? Is there no hope for her because her soul is gone?"

Will shook his head. "I hope not."

Olivia was about to say something when she noticed that Mitch had taken his shirt, shoes, and socks off, and was in the process of removing his pants; he thankfully left his boxers on.

"What are you doing?" She asked incredulously.

"Look," he said, his voice void of any shame. "I haven't showered for five days."

"The Sphere has only been here for three," Will commented.

"That's not the point," Mitch continued, unphased. "The point is I want a bath, and I'm going to take one." Without further comment, Mitch waded into the river and dunked himself under the water. He came back up and let out a loud whooping sound. "Refreshing!"

Will laughed and stood up. "Honestly, I could use one too."

Olivia couldn't deny that she also wanted to. She certainly wasn't doing it here, in front of these men. "That doesn't sound like a bad idea. I'm going to go on the other side of the bridge though. None of you follow me."

"Will you be ok," Will asked.

"I'll be fine," Olivia remarked, walking back the way they came to go around the bridge.

On the other side of the bridge, further down the river where she couldn't be seen, Olivia put her shotgun at the base of a tree. She stripped down and slipped into the water. It was cold, so she quickly slipped completely under the water rather than slowly suffering adjusting to the temperature. Mitch was right, the cool water was very refreshing, and it felt good to rinse herself in the water. She could hear the others in the water down the river, though they were out of her line of sight. She dunked her head under the water and rinsed her hair well. She wished she had thought of bringing soap and shampoo, but that would have to wait for another day. After finishing this, she climbed out of the water and used her flannel to dry off, then put the rest of her clothing on.

A pair of strong arms seized her from behind. An iron fist covered her mouth and the feeling of the muzzle of a gun being pressed against her temple prevented her from screaming out. "Make a sound, and we slaughter them like pigs," a harsh and cruel whispered into her ear. Olivia looked over her shoulder at the face of the man who was holding her. A pair of hateful yellow eyes belonging to Rick glared back at her, behind him were three others, they held knives and a hatchet in their hands. The gun that Rick held against her head was undeniably the one he had taken from Scott. "Understand? We will kill them if you make a sound."

Olivia quickly nodded her head.

"We should kill her now. Make her scream. Then the others, no waiting. Now! We do it now" the female rabid hissed.

"Yes, fill our stomachs with her, and them we will," one of the others agreed excitedly, all of them keeping their voices low.

"Quiet," Rick commanded. "Rage wants this one alive. Can't risk the others seeing. Have to fight them. We will take her."

"We can kill them quick, just take one bite," the female uttered.

"Challenge me again, and I will cut your tongue out," Rick snarled at her. "Bind her," he commanded. The female came up and wrapped a length of ripcord around Olivia's wrists, Staring into Olivia's eyes hatefully the entire time.

"We move, quietly," Rick commanded. Then began to drag Olivia to the base of the bridge. "Make a sound and we gut them. Remember." Olivia silently nodded again. Fear gripped her mind and her heart pounded in her chest. With Olivia in tow, they moved across the bridge, either they did not care about her shotgun, or they had not noticed it. They moved up the bridge, squeezing in between the wrecked cars. As they passed over the bridge, Olivia could hear her group in the water just a few dozen feet away, she could hear Will laughing. She closed her eyes at the situation she was in, cursing herself for not staying with the group.

"Kill them, we will," the female hissed at her again. Olivia nodded silently, tears beginning to stream down her face. Once on the other side, and over the second wall of vehicles at the base of the bridge. Rick roughly grabbed Olivia and threw her over his shoulder. All of them then began to run, Rick's shoulder digging painfully into Olivia's stomach as he ran. Behind her, the sound of her people, the sound of Will, faded away.

5

Rick, and the others with him, ran the entire distance to their camp, never stopping for a rest. Olivia's stomach was painfully sore from the trip, though the fear in her mind hardly made the pain noticeable now. All around her, yellow eyes looked at her hatefully, their teeth were bare, and they held knives, axes, hammers, and clubs. Many with dried blood on them. They gathered around, screaming incoherently, and extended their arms out, attempting to grab at her. Olivia couldn't help but scream at this horrid sight. It was a nightmare she couldn't escape, and no one seemed to be coming to help her. Rick swatted his arm at them and pointed Scotts pistol at them to wave them off. "She is not for you!" he shouted angrily at them.

Rick, and the crowd now following him, moved towards the large structure in the center of the camp. They passed the large bonfire in the center, the body still hung overhead, though much more of its flesh had been removed. The sick smell of burnt flesh filled Olivia's nose, she wanted to gag, wanted to scream, wanted to crawl in a hole and die all at once. With a swift motion, Rick threw Olivia to the ground. She landed hard and the force of the impact drove all the air out of her lungs. She lay on the ground, her hands still bound, gasping desperately to refill her lungs.

When she had gotten some semblance of control over her breathing again, she looked up at the large structure above her. It was haphazardly made from scraped wood and cut trees and had tarps extending over various points. In front of it stood many spikes driven into the ground, atop their tips were heads. Olivia squealed in horror at the recognition of one of them. It was Sheila, her mouth hanging open in a grotesque fashion. Next to her, on another spike, was the head of Scott. Olivia turned her head away in horror and let out a scream. The sound of laughter from the rabid filled the air around her.

"Recognize her, don't you?" Rick asked with mockery, kneeling beside her. "We found her in the woods, brought her here. Took some convincing, but she told us where you all were. More importantly, told us you were there. And told us where you were going. Rage was happy with her. So, he stopped her pain."

"What are you going to do to me?" Olivia asked, her voice a deep tremble.

"Not for me to decide," Rick said. He stood up and then called out in a loud voice. "Lord Rage, I have brought you your prize." He then kneeled in a bowing manner towards the large structure. As he did this, the devilish crowd around them fell silent and bowed down similarly.

For a moment, no one moved, and the air was completely still except for the sound of the roaring fire behind them. Footsteps sounded inside of the structure and a figure emerged from behind one of the hanging tarps that served as a sort of doorway. The figure wore a green army jacket, with dirty blue jeans, and large back combat boots. Calmly he stepped towards the hunched-over Olivia, a lead pipe, bloodied at the end hung from his hands.

Olivia froze with paralyzing horror and angst. She shook her head and cried, "No, no, no, no, no." The figure walked up to her and stood above her.

"Hi, Liv," Adam said with a smile, looking down at her from behind yellow eyes.

Seven

War

1

Olivia couldn't speak. She whimpered, her body trembling with a combination of fear and absolute hopelessness. From day one of this new world, her greatest hope, the thing driving her more than anything, was to find her brother. She had feared for his safety and had been willing to risk her own to find him. She had feared that he was dead - and that she would never find him again. Though her greatest fear, more than finding him dead, more than never knowing what happened to him, was to find him as something dark. Something twisted. Her brother, whom she loved very much, whom she had grown up with, whom she had endured the hardships of life with, had become her enemy, this had been the most unbearable possibility; one that had been circling her mind like a shark in bloody water. Now that fear was realized.

"I have brought you your prize, Lord Rage. Now, I want what you promised me," Rick said, still kneeling but now with his head up.

Adam, or Rage, Olivia still was shocked at the horrible transformation that had happened, didn't break his eye contact with Olivia. "Yes, it will be given to you."

"Both of them," Rick's voice was a mix of assertion and question.

"Yes, both your wife and daughter will be brought here. They will belong to you, and you may do with them what you want. They will be yours, and yours alone."

Olivia felt her fear and mind-numbing shock disappear for a moment at the mention of Rick's wife and daughter. It was Tiffany and Nina they were discussing. The thought of them being dragged here and given to Rick - who was horrible as a human and now one of these rabid animals - forced Olivia out of her state of shock. She was scared, her spirit was crushed, but regardless of this horror, she wanted to protect her friend.

Rick stood up, "How? How will my daughter and wife be given to me?"

Adam lifted his gaze from Olivia to the rest, he raised his voice loudly for the crowd. It was a voice that was different now than it had been when Olivia had last heard it, it was now more of a low metallic sound, grinding metal that promised pain. "I will send those of you who are strong and can fight to the camp of the weaklings, where you will kill those who resist and bring the rest back for us to have. Rick will lead you in this, and we will have what is ours back!" The yellow-eyed monsters in the crowd rose to their feet with a roar of approval. Screaming and raging, waving their weapons high into the sky in a craze of mad blood-lusted joy. Rick nodded in approval, a cruel snarl that curved into a sadistic smile on his face.

Adam pointed his bloody pipe at the severed head of Sheila. It was the same pipe that he had driven into Rick's belly the day the Sphere sang its song. "She told us that the camp is weak, they have few fighters and only a few weapons. They are weak, we are strong, they will be easy for you to take!" The rabid crowd roared again with approval.

Listening to these words, a horrible truth fell on Olivia. She knew the moment she had seen him walk out of the building saw his yellow eyes. It was a truth she had feared. Adam was, indeed gone, lost to this yellow-eyed rabid animal standing before her. However, this worked. Whatever the Sphere's song had done to him, Adam was gone, replaced by this, Lord Rage.

"What will you do with your captive," Rick called out, causing the crowd to fall silent, who shifted their hateful eyes to Olivia.

"She is mine," Adam announced loudly. "Mine and mine alone. No one is to harm her or to touch her. Or they will taste my rage!" He held the bloody pipe high in the air for all to see, this gesture produced a response of obedience from the crowd, many lowered their heads and averted their eyes. As if they were dogs who were being scolded by their master. Rick remained still. "I will keep her with me, and teach her to be as we are, to merge with her animal within. To rid herself of her inhibitions and her weakness. To be as strong and fierce as we are. To be free from the weakness of the old world. To take what she wants, to do what she wants. To be one with the animal!" The crowd roared again.

"What if you cannot?" Rick asked. Defiance was rich in his voice and his posture. The crowd fell silent again.

Adam grinned; yellow eyes fixed on Rick. He slowly strode towards Rick, his shoulders back and head high. As he approached, Rick's posture changed, he looked away and his head lowered. When Adam was standing in front of him, Rick knelt low. Like an animal being confronted by an alpha. Adam rested his pipe against Rick's cheek, leaving a crimson stain.

"How many times must you challenge me? When will you learn you, stubborn animal? She will submit," he spoke to Rick in that voice Olivia no longer recognized, he then turned his gaze to Olivia. They locked their eyes. "No matter how long it takes." Olivia closed her eyes, fighting back tears.

A loud explosion of shouting and commotion pulled Olivia out of the nightmare that she had been thrust into, and towards the group behind her. The rabid crowd scattered in a dizzy blur of motion as the spider charged into the center of the camp. Everyone, including Adam and Rick, scurried for cover, leaving Olivia still lying on the ground. The spider reared onto its hind legs and spread its front legs wide into the air, a low, almost purring-sounding hiss came out of him. His massive fangs extended outward and fidgeted in an aggressive and intimidating display. The Rabbids fled even further in fear.

"Get on, climb on me!" the spider shouted to Olivia.

Olivia immediately got to her feet, scurrying to the spider, gritting her teeth to push through the pain that gripped her body. The spider lowered its body flat to the ground, allowing Olivia to crawl up and sit on the space between the spider's head and abdomen, she gripped the long hairs as tightly as she could, albeit weakly, squeezing with her legs to hold on. Hurt and exhausted, she lay herself against the spider's body, her arms gripping with the little strength they had.

The spider moved forward with surprising speed and abruptness. The wind roared past Olivia, tossing her hair back in its tumultuous whirlwind. The spider, though moving quickly with its many legs flexing, still moved with complete silence, not even the sound of its many legs striking the ground could be heard. The only noise Olivia could hear was the sound of the air whipping past her.

The forest surrounding them whirled past quickly, a blur of green and brown that the spider moved through with ease and speed.

"Are you hurt?" the spider shouted back. Olivia looked up to see that there were eyes on either side of his head that seemed to be able to see her, as with the others, they were glazed over black and lidless, with no expression to be derived from them. Olivia shook her head, still unable to speak after her experience. The rushing winds slowed and stopped altogether as the spider came to a halt in the woods. Olivia breathed heavily. To her, it was the loudest sound in the world. Her whole body was still shaking, and her mind felt numb with all it had just experienced. "Olivia," the spider delicately said. "Is there anything I can do?"

"Take me back to the neighborhood, please." She could feel that she was on the verge of tears, she so very badly wanted to give in, to let herself wallow, to let herself scream in angry defiance of the situation she found herself and her brother in. However, she couldn't allow herself to break, not now. She had heard their plans to attack the camp, to take the people in it. Rick would take Tiffany and Nina. She continued, steeling herself. "We need to get my gun."

She rode the spider back to the river and found her shotgun leaning against the tree right where she had left it, the green canvas ammo pack was there, too.

"Are you sure it's a good idea for me to be seen?" the spider asked.

"The Rabid are coming to take everyone away and kill anyone who resists. We are going to need you to help us." As much as she was trying to push her fear away, it kept rising, choking her spirit and robbing her of her will to fight. Her hands were shaking again as she held the shotgun in her hands. She would have to use this soon. The shaking traveled up from her hands to her arms now. "What am I doing?" she whispered to herself, eyes beginning to water.

She felt a hairy appendage belonging to the spider rest softly on her shoulder. It had snuck up behind her, moving silently as it always had. She looked over her shoulder at the great spider. "You trusted me," it said to her. "I don't know why you did. But I'm grateful that you did. I'll trust your decision."

Her shaking had stopped, though her heart pounded in her chest. She looked up to the Sphere. "Give me strength."

2

"So, it can talk, but only you can hear it?" Mitch asked, the concern in his voice was plain.

"It's ok," Will chimed in. Taking a stance next to Olivia, who stood in front of the spider. "I met him last night, he's safe."

The spider stood at the edge of the camp in the Neighborhood, Olivia could tell by his posture that he was nervous, holding himself half behind his long legs as he had done before. Of course, the others didn't understand that this was a sign that he was nervous. When they had first arrived, screams and pointed weapons had been the first thing that welcomed him to the camp after he easily climbed over the hedge wall. If Olivia hadn't been riding on his back, waving her arms, and shouting for them not to shoot, he would have certainly been filled with bullet holes.

It was a good thing that she did. The timing of their return couldn't have been worse. Will and the others had just returned from the river, rushing back with the water after Olivia had disappeared by the bridge. They were in the process of telling everyone in the camp about Olivia's disappearance and arming themselves with weapons when a giant spider came silently crawling over the wall. After that quick standoff, and a great deal of reassurance to the people of the camp by Olivia, everyone was now standing in a wide semi-circle around the spider, Olivia, and Will. Although the rifles, shotguns, and pistols had all been lowered, the faces of the people were all still armed with concern and suspicion. The only one who didn't seem afraid was Megan's young son, who stood behind his mother's leg but looked at the spider with a sense of wonder.

"I'm sorry," Dr. Travis spoke up. "Are we just going to trust that this is a good idea? We already have a dangerous woman locked up in the shed, and now a giant spider who none of us can talk to unless the girl who speaks to demons is around?"

"Yep," Mr. Gregovski calmly said. "A giant spider that eats vampires, a giant turtle, a giant deer that scares away giant smoke monsters, all while we're being chased by yellow-eyed crazy people in a giant forest that grew overnight from a magic snowball from another world. I think I'll trust this."

"I trust Will, and Olivia," Tiffany chimed in, though her face still carried a worried look as she spoke. "If they trust him, then I do too."

"I don't want to overwhelm you, Olivia. But can you please tell me what's happening," the spider asked, his leg lifted up in the air.

"It's ok, they trust you," Olivia reassured him. "Isn't that right everyone," she called out to the crowd. The group nodded and made noises of agreement, though nervousness still seemed present in their demeanor. "Good, now that we have that out of the way. I have some bad news." Olivia recounted all that had happened, from the moment Rick grabbed her at the edge of the river, to when the spider had rescued her from the rabid camp. It pained Olivia to say it, but she even explained the conversation between Adam - now Lord Rage - and Rick, how he was coming with an army to take everyone away and keep Tiffany and Nina for himself. Tiffany's face was pale and fearful. She clutched Nina close, and Megan had come beside her to offer comfort. "I'm so sorry, Tiffany," Olivia concluded sincerely.

Tiffany only nodded quietly, her gaze was cast down to the ground and her face bore a weighty worry and concern that words themselves could never convey. Megan spoke up, "What are we going to do?"

An uneasy quiet fell on the group. People looked at one another, desperate for some answer. Tiffany's gaze remained down at the ground, to Olivia, it appeared as if she had accepted her horrid fate. As if she were a death row inmate, with no hope of a stay of execution, waiting for the call to walk to her final moments in life, unable to alter her destiny. Will seemed to react to this.

"We fight." The clearness in his voice broke the heavy air that surrounded them all. Tiffany looked up, a hopeful expression taking its place on her face. "We know that they are coming, we know their plan, and there may be more of them, but we are better armed than they are, Olivia told us that they have only handheld weapons, we have an advantage that way. We also have this place," Will nodded his head to their surroundings. "They would have to try hard to get over the hedge wall, that's an extra line of defense. And, besides," Will turned to face the spider, "I'm sure our new friend would help us fight."

After Olivia translated this to him, the spider lowered and raised its head in a nodding motion. The motion was awkward, but the message was clear enough for all to understand. The spider would fight with them.

"Dope," Mitch muttered. "Pet tarantula for the win."

"Wolf spider," Mr. Gregovski rebutted.

"What," Mitch asked.

"That's not a tarantula, he's a wolf spider."

"What's the difference?"

"The differences are huge; Wolf spiders are ambush hunters that-"

"So, what's our plan," Olivia asked, interrupting the conversation before time was wasted. "We don't have much time."

"Right," Will began. "Obviously, we are the safest here. The problem is this area is large, perhaps too large for us to defend. We only have a few who can fight. Besides, Rick knows the area, and Olivia said that she saw him here on the first day."

"He and Adam both came from this neighbor-hood, it's possible they may even know about the small hole in the hedge wall, after all, they were both in here when the Sphere changed everything."

"Right," Will continued, "So, they will be coming for the wall. Knowing that we are positioned inside of here. So, we hit them early, take them by surprise, and fight them somewhere outside of the wall. My guess is they will take the road to get here. If we hit them somewhere between here and the bridge, catch them out in the open, we can take them. They called us all weak, I'm guessing they don't think we are ready to fight, they probably assume we are hiding behind the hedge. If things go badly, we can still use this as a fallback area, keeping all those who won't fight in here.``

"You can't just leave us here while you go out and fight," Megan pleaded.

"A few of us can stay behind, just in case," Tim suggested.

"Yes, in fact, you will probably have to bring the wounded back here, I can stay back to treat them," Dr.

Travis added. Olivia felt annoyed by this. To her, it seemed that he was just trying to avoid any danger.

"You would do the most good at the battle, Travis," Will replied. "Where the wounded will be."

The spider raised his leg, "I can continue scouting around, when they head this way, I can return and let you all know." Olivia, who had been quietly translating the conversations between everyone the best she could for the spider, repeated what he had said for the group.

"That's perfect, thank you," Will said.

"They could leave at any time, I should go keep an eye on them now," the spider said, which Olivia translated for the group before he turned and silently left, disappearing over the hedge wall.

3

Night had descended on the camp and the perimeter fires were lit, though the spider had not returned with news of the enemies' movements, the heaviness of the air hugged thicker than the smoke rising from the flames. No one slept, no one rested, there was no guitar and singing that night, only the weight of what was to come. Tiffany, Nina, Morgan, and her kids had all gone to the garage of Olivia's house again. Some of the men, including Will had taken up post to guard it. Olivia had taken up sitting by herself next to a fire, her weapon next to her and ready. She wasn't expecting them to come tonight, not with the crawlers in the woods. No, she was sure the enemy would come tomorrow.

Olivia shook her head bitterly. The enemy. That was who her brother had become. All this time that she had been looking for him, she had been living in fear. Little did she know, she had been living in fear of him.

Lord Rage. The image of Scott's body being carried into the building while the rabid mob chanted "Rage, Rage, Rage," was sitting in her mind. Now, she knew who they were chanting for. Her brother. Her brother whom she had grown up with. Her brother who put people in cages. Her bother who killed. Her bother who plotted her enslavement.

He was always angry when he was younger, after Mom had left. In many ways, he was the classic chip-on-your-shoulder guy, and it made him hard to approach. In many ways, Olivia had lived in somewhat fear of him the past few years. Not fear that he would lash out and hurt her, but rather fear that she would do something to upset him and that he would then abandon her. It wasn't fair. She had, and still did resent him for that. She lost Mom too, how come he got to be moody and angry at her expense when she too was suffering? Even after Dad died, he stayed in his room, stayed unapproachable, stayed distant. Sure, he helped when she had the accident that confined her to that awful leg brace and the house, but even then, she felt trapped. One wrong word and she would be truly alone.

Looking back, now, Olivia felt that she could see that it was always there, the anger. The rage. The Sphere, with its transforming song, had just brought it out for all to see. Perhaps, he had been so practiced at containing the hate, the resentment, the anger, that when the Sphere brought it out, he had already learned to control it. That's why he seemed so calm compared to the others. He had practiced it. He truly was Lord Rage, the lord of his rage. Now, he was lord over the host of animalistic rabid, yellow-eyed freaks. He spoke about being set free, letting the animal out. Is that what he wanted, all these years of isolating, and sulking? To let his anger and his rage out?

All these years, all this time. Rage had been lurking underneath.

Her mind was swimming and reminiscing about her and her brother's life together. Signs of this darkness that had been in him seemed to be everywhere. Her skin crawled when she thought of the smile he had, looking at her with his yellow eyes. If there was to be any solace in this situation, it was that he didn't want to hurt her, nor would he allow anyone else to hurt her. Rather, he wanted her for himself. To teach her to embrace the animal. *To be like we are*, he said. Olivia shuddered. She knew that that could never happen. She could never condone the behavior, the violence, the cruelty that they had. What terrified her even more was that Adam probably didn't care. She would submit to him, however long it takes. That was the word he used, submit.

Her father was half Ho-Chunk Native American, and he would occasionally travel up to Black River Falls to help his brother with breaking and training horses to later sell at auction. They would put the young horse in a pen and drive it around in circles as someone stood in the center. This would last for as long as it took to make the animal recognize the dominance of the person in the center. Then, the person in the center would walk to the edge of the pen, look away, and hold their hand out behind them. If the horse came up to them and sniffed their hand, they were submitted to them. Their spirit was broken. That's what it means when they say a horse is "broken in," it's their spirit that's broken. That way, they can be ridden. If the horse didn't do this, then the process would start again and again.

Her father had taken her and her brother to this process of submitting a horse more than once, and she would often ask her father how long this would take, or how many times they needed to do this. As long as it takes, is what he would tell her. Now, her brother was using this same language about her. She would submit to him, as long as it took. Olivia was no longer in a place where she wanted to cry and break down over this. That seemed to have passed now. No, now there was a hardness to her. There were five stages to grief, and denial had come and gone now, she supposed she was in anger. That was good, given the war that was coming. Olivia looked up to the Sphere. At night, it took on a pale gray glow, probably light reflecting, or something of the sort, she guessed. The moon, waxing, yet still relatively full shined brightly in the sky with it. She stared at the Sphere, anger rising at it.

Why? Why did it heal me, and not him? It only heals physical wounds, not the emotional ones left by being abandoned by your mother. And, if that is the case, why not? It could fix her leg, turn the town into a forest, and bring back the dead and make them immortal. Why couldn't it heal his hatred and anger? Why did it have to turn him into this? *Did it turn him though*, she asked herself. Rather, it seems like all it did was let out what was already there.

"How do I help him," she whispered up at the Sphere. "How do I help all of them? Adam, the spider, Melody, any of them. How?" She could feel it in her chest, she could feel that she needed to help them, somehow. She had to. "How?"

The noise of someone walking pulled Olivia out of her mind and to Mr. Gregovski, who was casually strolling over to where the shed that held Melody was. He spotted Olivia, sitting next to the fire, and arched his path wide to the left so that he would pass by her.

"Can't sleep," he stated to her. "Figured I'd give the guy watching the girl a break."

"You don't have a gun," Olivia observed, being careful that her voice did not show any sign of the struggle she was having.

"That's ok, I suppose I'll have to borrow the one from him, then."

"Ok," Olivia replied, she couldn't see the shed or the man who was currently guarding it from here. "Be careful." Mr. Gregovski gave her a thumbs-up gesture and resumed on his way. He seemed to have a sure stride in his step, like a man on a mission. Olivia considered it for a moment, then returned to her thoughts.

She looked at the shotgun that had been her father's. He had taken her hunting, camping, and hiking many times, and often, this weapon accompanied them on their trips together. Would she be expected to take this family heirloom of theirs, raise it in anger, and kill her brother with it? She hated the thought and hated even more that the horrible thought could come to pass. Could she even do it? Could she kill Adam if she had to? Olivia wasn't sure. She felt confident that, if she needed to, she could kill Rick. Especially if she needed to protect Tiffany and Nina from him.

Olivia watched as one of the men of the group walked past, away from where the shed was. It must have been the person who Mr. Gregovski had replaced. Olivia looked to see if he was still carrying a weapon but was unable to see in the dark before he traveled out of sight. Olivia shut her eyes and took a deep breath. She needed to sleep. Likely, the fight would happen tomorrow. She needed her strength for this.

Olivia woke up still lying next to the fire. The soft warm light of the morning chased away the feeling of tiredness that had taken her at some point in the night. She sat up, and stretched, the smell of smoke and burnt ash filling the air around her. Some distance away, near the base of the giant tree, Olivia saw that there was a small group of people standing in a huddle and talking excitedly. Will was with them. She lumbered up and headed over to the group to see what the commotion was about.

Will noticed Olivia walking up to him. "Liv," he said excitedly, "You have to see this!"

"What's going on," she asked.

"It's Melody, look."

Standing there, next to Will, was Melody. She no longer had the void stare that the crawlers had, her skin was no longer that sickly ashen gray color, the bags under her eyes had disappeared and she was no longer reacting violently to the light of the day. Rather, she stood solemnly, her eyes calm and alive. Her skin did seem a shade paler, and her hair had gone from its bright blond to a whiter silver, but she was awake and aware. "What happened?" Olivia asked in wonder. A new spirit welled up inside her at the sight of a restored Melody.

"I think I may be able to answer that," a voice said. Olivia looked at the younger man who had just spoken. He appeared to be in his mid-thirties. Taller. With dark hair and eyes, he had a very familiar smile on his face and Olivia felt that she recognized him yet couldn't place it.

"Who are you?" she asked the man.

"It's me, Olivia," he said with a smile, his dark eyes bright. "Lew, Lewis Gregovski, and it wasn't me who did this," he said, turning to face the massive tree that stretched up to the sky behind them. "It was the tree."

4

"I don't quite know how to explain it," The young Lewis Gregovski, whom Olivia felt that she was meeting for the first time, began. "I knew there was something special to the tree the moment I saw it when we crossed the river that day. I was hurting, tired and hungry. I had hoped that this new world would be good, after the Sphere had taken my cancer away. But between the yellow-eyed people kidnapping us, and the death of your friend while you all came to save us, I had my doubts that it was a good thing it came. But I felt, looking at the tree that day, that there was indeed something good here. As if the light that I had spent all this time looking for had finally arrived, and it was in the tree, somehow."

"When that thing: that spirit or monster, or whatever it was left Melody and made her one of the crawlers, well, I felt I had to do something to help her. I didn't know what at the time. Then, last night, as I was trying to sleep, I felt a voice, or a presence, or something speak to me…" Lew shook his head, "No, not like that. It was more like some kind of message, or truth appeared in my heart. I don't know how else to explain it, I just knew this truth somehow. I think either the Sphere or the tree itself just revealed this to me."

Olivia and Will looked at one another, both knowing exactly what he was talking about. They had experienced it themselves. In fact, they all had.

"I think we all have experienced that," Dr. Travis said. "We all know, somehow, that the thing in the sky isn't some kind of alien spaceship, but something alive instead." Others nodded and murmured in agreement with this statement.

"Exactly," Lewis continued. "Anyway, last night I felt that if I made Melody touch the tree - just touch it, she would be redeemed." He paused for a moment contemplatively. "It's a strange word; redeemed. But that's the word that comes to mind."

"That's the word I would use too," Melody said. It was the first time that Olivia had heard her voice since changing back. Her voice sounded different. Before, she had seemed immature, whiny, and a bit head-in-the-clouds. Now, she seemed peaceful and contemplative, as if the experience had somehow grown her in years. Her spirit seemed older now, wiser, and more mature, though her appearance - apart from the hair - seemed to remain the same. It wasn't just her voice that communicated this, but it was everything about her. She had changed. Somehow.

"So," Mr. Gregovski continued. "That's what I did. I got up, and walked past you, Olivia. Then, after dismissing the gentleman who was watching the shed, I went up and opened it. She came out and jumped on me immediately, sinking her teeth in and latching onto my arm," Mr. Gregofski revealed a healed scar on his harm. It had obviously been made by a set of teeth. "She latched on with a strength that I would never have thought capable of from a girl her size, she stayed clamped on, sucking the blood that was coming out of me. I knew that I didn't have long, I'm an old man after all. Well, was, an old man. Anyway, I decided to start moving towards the tree, she didn't fight me on this, she just walked with me, staying latched on the whole time, but walking with me. Drinking the blood was more important than where we were going, I suppose. I felt weak by the time I led her to the tree, so I just pointed her to it and then made her step into it. Pushing her so that her back was completely flat against it. She let go of me then. Good thing, too, I had no strength in me anymore and fell to the ground when she did."

Mr. Gregovski looked at Melody, "Then she changed, she took in a deep breath, her color came back to her skin, her hair changed to that white color."

Olivia looked at Melody, "Do you remember any of this?"

Melody shook her head, "The last thing I remember was the voice leaving my body the day we were in the field."

"The voice?" Dr. Travis asked.

"You mean that thing that came out of you?" Tiffany asked.

"I don't know about that thing, I didn't see it," Melody commented.

"That's ok," Will said, his voice a reassurance: "Just tell us what you remember, from the beginning."

Melody took a deep breath, then began. "I first heard the voice when I was in the woods, back at our old camp by the river, one day when I was trying to get my phone working. It came from around me, out of the air, not out of the phone. The phone didn't even turn on. I asked the voice to help me, to save me. The voice told me that there was no help coming and that it would help me if I let it. It told me that I needed to open my mind to it, and that it would show me how to be saved, that it would enlighten me and set me free."

Melody shook her head as she remembered. "So, I let it in me. From then on, the voice was inside me. It told me that I needed to keep it a secret, that if I told anyone about it, it would leave me and I would never be saved, I would never be free. It would whisper things to me, tell me that it was god, and that I needed to worship it. I would ask when it was going to help me, and it would tell me that I needed to give more of myself to it. So, I did. It would always promise me things, promise to save me, to make me strong, but it never did. It only took. The more of me it took, the worse I felt. I started to become hungry and confused. The more I gave it, the more it took, and the more confused I became. The day we moved camp, I felt like there was nothing left of me, and there was no more room inside of me for me. The space inside of me belonged to him now, and I was slipping into darkness. Before I left, the voice was mocking me, telling me I was nothing and that I didn't matter. That I was worthless, and it needed me gone. Before I slipped away and fell into darkness, I asked who the voice was. Who it really was. It told me its name was Ichmir."

Ichmir, so that thing had a name, Olivia thought to herself.

Melody's eyes teared up, "I felt like I was in that darkness for so long. I know it was only a day or two, but for me… I thought it would never end. I've never felt so alone, and so sad in my life. I even tried to just remember what happiness felt like, tried to think of a happy memory that I had had, so I could just remember what it was once like to feel good, but I couldn't. I was in this black void where there was no joy or anything good, only sorrow and loneliness. It felt endless, like there was no such thing as time."

"Then, I saw the light, it grew brighter and warmer, and felt hope again, the light filled me with peace and love, with a warmth that I can't explain. The light took on the shape of a tree. I felt myself being drawn to it. That's when I woke up, I was on the ground. Next to Mr. Gregovski. Next to the tree."

"Please, call me Lew," he commented. "Mr. Gregovski sounds so old now," Lew, had a playful smile on his face as he said this. Olivia couldn't help but smile.

"That doesn't explain how you got younger though," Dr. Travis interjected. "Or how your wounds healed, not to mention how you recovered from the blood loss."

"Yes, of course," Lew said. "When I pushed Melody into the tree, I had collapsed against the tree. I had the strangest sensation like, oil was being pushed out of my body and leaking out through my pores. I even looked at my arms to see if anything was coming out of me. I didn't see anything, but I realized that my skin was tightening on my arms. My skin was becoming smooth, and the wrinkles were fading away. I felt strength returning to me. When the light of dawn came, I realized what had happened. That we both were healed."

Everyone in the group listened in amazement. A few reached out and tentatively touched the tree, though nothing seemed to have happened. Olivia's mind raced. "Do you think it will work on others?" She asked Lew, with cautious hope. "Fix them? Or redeem them, as you said?"

"Yes," Melody said, her voice quick and definitive.

Will looked at Olivia curiously, eyes narrowed. "What are you thinking, Liv?"

Olivia felt tears forming in her eyes, "this may be a way to save Adam."

Before Olivia could explain further, Tiffany let out a startled scream, which jarred everyone out of their reverie. The spider that had silently crawled up to the group.

"They are coming," The spider exclaimed, and Olivia translated his message to the rest of the group.

"When, and how many?" Will asked.

"The majority of the camp, they left this morning."

"Is my brother with them?" Olivia asked. "He's the leader, green jacket and blue jeans, with a lead pipe."

"I did not see him." The spider answered. "The other one is leading them."

"Rick," Olivia stated grimly.

5

The quiet before a battle is the loudest sound in the world, Olivia thought to herself as she crouched behind a vehicle on the long road to the bridge. That phrase sounded good to her, and she turned it over and over in her mind. She used to write poems when she was younger, and even tried to write songs, mostly when she was sitting in class bored. She had a notebook that was only for her writings, and kept it a closely guarded secret that only she knew about. Not that others were trying, mind you, but the mind of a young girl is a secretive place and that notebook had been filled with her deepest thoughts and feelings. Now, she crouched behind a car, holding her father's shotgun, waiting for an enemy to come. How much had changed. How simple those times had been.

Will was crouched next to her. After the spider had reported the incoming hostility, they all scrambled to get their weapons and ammunition. Will had tried to tell Olivia that she shouldn't come, even trying to tell her to stay back and protect the others. Olivia protested and reminded Will that they needed the numbers, and that only she could speak to the spider.

They had nearly ran the entire way to this place, and now they waited. Still, the exchange between her and Will bothered her, she needed an answer.

"Why did you try and tell me to stay?" She asked.

Will paused for a moment before answering. "When we couldn't find you by the river, I thought you were dead. I can't tell you how distraught I was. When you came back, I was so relieved. I care about you, Liv. I hate the idea of something happening to you. This may sound weird, but I feel like I have a second chance with you. I failed to be there for my daughter, I can't fail you, too."

Olivia touched Will's arm, "I know, Will. But there's too much at stake."

"You have no idea how much it kills me to know that I was right there when they were taking you. Splashing in the water like some idiot. I should have done something."

"I know, but that's how I feel now. They are coming, and they want to hurt our friends, the people we care about. I can't just sit back in safety and not try. I can't. I have to be here, Will."

Will relented his position, and now, Olivia, Will, Dr. Travis, Mitch, Tim, the Spider, and the two other men from the group that Olivia hadn't met yet were out here. Ready to defend their new home, and the people in it. Lewis had wanted to come, and even Melody said she was willing, but Dr. Travis had forbidden them. He stated that they didn't yet know what side effects the healing process of the tree would have on them, and that the battlefield was the last place he wanted to have to deal with any potential issues. Lewis had protested, but in the end, it was decided that Lewis would stay behind and protect the others if anything were to happen.

So, here they were. A team of seven, against a savage mob, hellbent on slavery and death. Yes, they were armed, yes, they were prepared, but they were certainly outnumbered. The spider had described a group of fifty or more. Not to mention that they didn't have fighting experience, except for Will. True, the other side probably didn't either, but they were rabid. Their ferocity was all the training and experience they would need. And soon, that ferocity would be bearing down on this rag-tag group of survivors.

Dr. Travis joined them behind the car. "Everyone is ready."

Will, Olivia, and Dr. Travis were in the center, while two of the others were off the edges facing into the open area ahead of them. Together, they made what was called a "kill box," the plan was that the other two members of their group, who were not set up with in the box, would draw the enemy force into this open space that lay before them. Then, they would then open fire from multiple directions. The rabids would have three choices: flee, stay and try fighting, or charge at the firing line. If any stragglers or members of the rabid group tried to depart, the spider would snatch them up. This plan seemed good. As long as the approaching forces took the bait and entered the kill box.

Olivia felt as if time were moving in slow motion. The calm that surrounded her was, indeed, beautiful. Birds were chirping, the sun was high in the sky, and the day was warm. A soft breeze had been coming and going, cooling them at seemingly just the right moments. However, knowing what would be coming, the calm and the setting felt more eerie than anything else.

"Where are they?" Dr. Travis whispered urgently.

As if in response to the doctor's question, the pop of two shots ringing out sounded off, and Olivia's heart began to pound in response. She took a deep breath, steeling herself for what was to come.

"It's in the wrong place," Will said. His voice filled with concern. He was right, the shots came from far to the left, at that angle, the group wouldn't come into the kill box, but would rather enter it from behind one of the flanks. If they stayed where they were, the group would be facing the wrong direction, if they only pivoted to face the coming enemy, then they wouldn't be standing in between them and the Town. "We need to move, now." Will jumped up and ordered the group to move, they got up and quickly moved far to the left, positioning themselves between the Town and where it sounded like the gunfire came from. They reorganized, and created a firing line. The position seemed strong, they had cover and a good line of sight. However, they were now aimed at the line of trees that had grown up around the edge of the road, meaning that the enemy, when they came out of this tree line, would also have cover.

"Not exactly a kill box," Olivia remarked to Will.

"No, it isn't," Will replied. "But we still have the road dividing the forest here, they can't cross to the Town unless they cross the road."

"Won't we be only holding them off then? The original plan was to take them out."

"They're coming," a voice from the tree line shouted. Tyler, who had been one of the men who were in charge of leading the rabids here came running from the tree line.

"Over here," Will called to him.

Tyler turned his head in surprise, and Will called again. Tyler changed his course and ran to where Will was. "They got Bruce," he said breathlessly. "They didn't come up the road, they came through the woods."

The Spider joined them, coming out of the tree line farther down to the left, but moved directly towards them. Olivia assumed that this had to do with his senses, that he had known they moved their position before he even exited the trees. "They moved across the river first, then cut through the woods. They are almost here." Olivia translated his words.

"Stick to the original plan," Will said to the spider. "Keep them bunched up in the woods, don't let them spread out too much or we won't be able to hold this line." After Olivia relayed this information, the spider quickly, and silently, disappeared into the woods.

Olivia looked around at the group, they were now down to six, plus the spider. She had a bad feeling about this.

"They will have cover, so make your shots count," Will announced to the others.

An animalistic screech sounded off from the tree line, followed by several shots. Olivia looked to see a female rabid, she was screaming at the top of her lungs, charging towards the firing line with a hammer held high above her head. Mitch fired a few shots at her, and she was stumbling in her steps. A third round ripped through her hard, and she flopped down to the road.

It had begun. Numerous rabid came out of the tree line, running with fierce intensity, yellow eyes glaring with hatred. "Open fire!" Will shouted. The line exploded with gunfire, dropping many of the oncoming onslaught to the ground. Olivia aimed at a man with a wifebeater and blue jeans, pulling the trigger of the shotgun that had been her father's, the man was spun around by the buck-shot and fell to the broken concrete beneath. She chambered another round. She hadn't been sure if she was able to do this, to kill her enemy, but it seemed the need for survival had overcome her fear. She fired again, and again. Monstrous enemies falling with each shot.

The Mossberg 500 that Olivia held carried 5 shells in its tube, with an additional one in the chamber if one chose to load it that way. On the side of the shotgun was a nylon shell carrier that sported six additional shells. She also had her green canvas ammo bag that held around fifty additional 12-gauge shells inside. The Mossberg was more than sufficient to take down one of the enemies with a single shot, the problem was that loading a shotgun was a slow process. She had already burned through half of the rounds loaded into her gun and would need to reload in only three more shots. The shell carrier on the side meant she didn't have to dig in the ammo bag yet, but that would surely come, soon. However, with six other guns barking death at the incoming enemy, Olivia's' fire wasn't the only one holding the horde back.

The first wave of attackers was brought down quickly by this volley of fire, and now lay on the road in front of them in heaps. The remaining Rabbid forces seemed to have understood the position and remained in the cover provided by the tree line.

Tyler stood up, a triumphant sound in his voice, "what's the matter," he taunted. "Where are your cages now, huh?" A shot rang out from the enemy side, and the distinct sound of a bullet whizzed past Tyler, he immediately dove back down to cover. A quick volley of fire erupted from the tree line, bullets impacting the car they were hiding behind. It was clear that it was more than one weapon firing.

"Stay down!" Will shouted out to the others. "They have guns!"

"I thought you said they only had the one from that guy they killed," Dr. Travis remarked incredulously to Will and Olivia.

"I only saw the one they took from Scott," Olivia replied, now loading her shotgun with shells from the bag. She decided to leave the shells in the carrier alone for now.

Will shook his head. "It was stupid of us to assume that they wouldn't have any."

A standstill of sorts had broken out, they traded shots here and there, but, for the most part, both sides hunkered down behind their respective covers, neither moving. Watching from behind the car, Olivia could see the bunches of rabid moving and peeking out behind the cover. At one point, a group of them moved to the right and began to form a group at the edge of the rabids line.

"They're trying to flank us, on the right," Will cried out. Through the trees, Olivia saw the spider dash out and rear up on its legs, snatching one of the rabid and dragging it away kicking and screaming as it dangled in its long fangs. The others recoiled and shouted curses at the spider, this seemed to draw much of the rabids attention. They attempted to fire on the spider, but he moved quickly, pulling another one of them into the brush and out of sight. The spider continued his assault, reappearing and snatching another, whisking him away up a tree where he again disappeared, moving from tree to tree to avoid their fire.

Far to the left of the line, opposite where the spider was doing his work and far down the road away from the battle, Olivia thought she saw three figures cross the road and disappear into the brush. It happened so fast that she wasn't sure she had seen it.

"Will, I think I saw a few cross the road down that way!" Olivia shouted over the firing line.

"Are you sure?" Will replied, still looking through his rifle scope, then taking a shot and dropping a rabid whose head was above cover.

Olivia wasn't sure, "I think so, it may be Rick, trying to get to the town!"

Will looked at the firing line, and the tree line with desperation, "We can't leave! If we retreat now, this whole force will descend on the town."

"I know, you and the others stay and keep them here. I'll go."

"Like hell you will."

"Will, you need to stay back, there won't be enough of us here to hold them off if you come."

Will looked at Olivia desperately, shaking his head. "Will, I'm doing this. Please trust me."

For a moment, Will's face remained unyielding, then softened and he nodded. "Leave the ammunition bag, we may need the rounds if we are here for too long."

Olivia nodded, then hugged Will quickly. Before saying another word, Olivia began running in the direction of the hedge wall entrance. Keeping her head down to avoid catching a bullet in the back of the head.

Her lungs were burning by the time she reached the hole in the hedge wall, still, she pushed through the exhaustion and crawled through the hole, emerging on the other side. She exited the other side to discover Lewis lying on the ground. A group of people were gathered around him. A rabid lay dead next to him.

"What happened?" Olivia asked, running up to the group.

"Three of them came in, I got one, but one of the others shot me in the back of the shoulder," Lewis said.

"Where did he go?" Olivia asked, already knowing the answer.

Lewis pointed towards where her house was. Where Tiffany, Nina, and the others were. Olivia groaned with dismay and ran to the house, she found Melody leaning against the garage door, holding her head. There was blood in her white hair. "One of them hit me from behind," she reported, her voice was groggy.

Olivia ran around the edge of the building and into the door of the garage. Inside, Megan was comforting Tiffany, who was crying hard and shaking. "He took her! He took her!" she screamed when Olivia entered. "He took Nina! Rick took Nina!"

The sound of gunshots drew Olivia out and to the hedge wall. Running outside and towards the sound, Olivia found a rabid dead on the ground and a group of survivors standing next to a hole in the hedge. "He took her through here," they franticly shouted to her. "He threatened to kill her if we followed. He came so fast, we didn't have time."

Olivia pushed through the hole in pursuit. Emerging out on the other side, Olivia was able to see places where the grass had been ruffled, she continued to pursue it. Olivia broke out into a run in this direction, looking down from time to time to see the parted grass. She soon came to the open field where the grass was long. This was the same field where the thing called Ichmir had come out of Melody. Off to her left, the pond with the turtle sat. She was panting heavily by the time she arrived here, and her legs threatened to no longer cooperate with her quest.

She scanned the horizon and didn't see any figures in the distance. She continued to follow the trail, which was even easier to see now, in this long grass. It was moving close to the pond, and Olivia continued to run at full speed. Her lungs and legs burning with soreness. It was near the pond itself, where the length of the grass was much shorter, yet still able to show that it had been trampled recently, that Olivia noticed the trail suddenly veered hard to the right, away from the pond. Olivia stopped for a moment and followed the trail with her eyes. It continued curving hard to the right, in a wide arc that then doubled back on itself. Olivia gasped when she realized what this meant.

Olivia's back shoulder exploded with pain, as did her back on the left side and her right thigh below the hip. She felt the ribs on her left side shatter with the impact of the bullet as three quick shots from a pistol being fired behind her rang out. Olivia felt the air being driven from her chest as she fell to the ground. Olivia tried to get up, gasping desperately but the pain made it unbearable to stand.

"Had to, didn't you?" the unmistakable voice of Rick called out from behind her. "Lord Rage wouldn't have hurt you; he would have treated you well. If you only submitted."

Olivia twisted in pain to face Rick, who stood pointing Scott's gun at her. He held Nina against himself. His hand was over her mouth. Tears were running down her face. Olivia's shotgun lay on the ground where she had dropped it, about four feet away, but it might as well have been four miles away.

"I learned I had to do that. Submit. He was stronger than me and beat me with the pipe when we first woke up after the Sphere had done its work. But he treated me well if I obeyed him. Didn't want to, had to. So, I came up with a plan. Get my worthless brat and wife back, then I'll have an heir, make my own family. Then we will kill him, and I will replace him when he dies. I will be the new Lord then." Rick tapped the gun to the side of his head. "I'm smart. Then you came. Ruined my plans. I had to do this to get the brat. Not to worry, we will be back with more, and we will get all of you then. For now, I'll take this one with me, raise her in our ways. It will be hard, she's too soft now. That can be beaten out of her though. The other one is no good, the whore, just damaged goods. I was hoping to make more with her. Ones that would be free and wild like us, not weak and pathetic like them. But I will settle for this one."

Olivia tried to speak but couldn't. The pain in her side was too great. She could still breathe, which told her that the bullet had not entered or pierced her lung. But the pain of breathing was beyond description. She was feeling lightheaded, the bullet wound on her thigh was leaking blood quickly, despite the pressure she was applying to it. She could barely raise her voice above a whisper.

Rick walked closer to her; the gun still pointed at her. "What, what do you have to say? Before I kill you. I'll think of an excuse later, to explain your death to Lord Rage."

"It… it… it will be ok… Nina," Olivia was finally able to utter, looking at little Nina, who still had tears streaming down her face.

Rick shook his head, a disgusted look on his face. "Pathetically weak," he uttered. Then pushed the gun against Olivia's temple.

"Rick!" a female voice called out loud from behind Rick. Rick turned and stepped to the other side of Olivia, putting her in between him and the voice.

Olivia was surprised to see Tiffany standing there in the field, eyes locked on Rick, a large rock in her hand. Rick let out a sinister laugh. "Look at this," he mocked.

"Shut up, Rick!" Tiffany snapped back. This sudden display of confidence caught Rick off guard. "Let her go and take me with you instead. I won't fight you. I won't try to escape, I'll go willingly, and you can make all these heirs that you're talking about. I'll even help you raise them, how you want them to be raised. Just let Nina go, and I will be yours."

Olivia tried to protest, but the pain and weakness wouldn't allow her to do any more than whisper. Rick let out a bitter laugh, "Why? why would you do that?"

"Because you sacrifice for the people you love, that's what you do. You never understood that, Rick. We got pregnant young, you had to give up your college dream. And you spent the rest of your life drinking and feeling sorry for yourself, blaming us. You hated us for it. We have to sacrifice things for the people we love, well, I'm willing to sacrifice myself for her. So, take me instead.'

Rick glared at her for a moment, hatred in his yellow eyes. He then let out another long, drawn-out, horrible laugh. "Fine, fine. It will be like old times, babe. Only, you have to listen to me. Do what I say. Let me do whatever I want."

"You act like it wasn't that way before, Rick. But I'll do whatever. Just let her go."

"Fine," Rick said, then he let go of Nina. Nina slowly started to walk towards her mom.

"Nina, I need you to help Olivia, she's hurt."

"But Mom, Mom, please," Nina pleaded, tears still streaming from her eyes.

"Nina, please, kneel down, and help Olivia," Tiffany's words were slow and deliberate. As if she had chosen them carefully and wanted them followed exactly.

Nina stepped over to Olivia slowly.

"Kneel down and help her," Tiffany said in the same slow voice.

Nina knelt down by Olivia. The moment Nina had done this, Tiffany drew her arm back and hurtled the rock that she had been holding at Rick, it flew right by his head and past him, landing with a loud splash in the pond that

Olivia didn't realize was now right behind him after he had stepped around her to face Tiffany.

Rick had stepped back to get out of the missile's path, he now looked at Tiffany with shock. He laughed again. "Even in this new world, you're still worthless and pathetic. Can't even throw a rock right. But don't worry, I'll make you useful."

The water in the pond churned for a moment, drawing Rick's attention away. "What-" Rick said. The water in the pond heaved up as the head of the massive snapping turtle launched out of its murky depths. Its jaws open wide, and its long neck extended out, turning sideways, and snatching Rick up in its hooked maw. Rick let out a scream of horror and anger, the turtle's jaws closed tighter, and Olivia could hear ribs and bones breaking. Rick's scream turned into a high-pitched moan as the turtle slipped back and pulled him beneath the water. For a moment, Tiffany stood staring at the water that was settling back down, her face was stern and resolved.

She then moved to Olivia, she took off the long-sleeved shirt that she had on over a tank top and pressed it against Olivia's thigh. Olivia felt herself slipping away, the pain seemed to have stopped, and she was feeling tired. "Olivia, stay with me!" Tiffany said. Olivia's vision started to blur, and she could no longer keep her eyes open. Her eyes fell shut, she could still hear, though everything sounded far away.

Olivia heard what seemed like the sound of footsteps approaching them.

"Who are you?" Tiffany demanded.

"I only wish to help," a soft, and comforting male voice replied.

"Wait, what are you?" Tiffany asked, just before Olivia slipped into unconsciousness.

Eight

Confrontation

1

Olivia woke with a gasp. Her eyes opened to a view of the inside of one of the large tents. She was on one of those folding camping cots, a comfortable pillow under her head and a blanket laid out over her.

"Liv, can you hear me?" Will asked.

Olivia nodded.

"Are you feeling ok?" he asked.

"I think so," Olivia said. Feeling a little confused at the fact that she did. She moved the blanket over and looked at her thigh, there was a round scar in the place where the bullet had struck her. She reached back and touched her shoulder, feeling a similar scar on her back. She then realized she was only in her underwear but had the blanket covering her.

"How-?" she asked.

"The tree," Will replied.

"It's going to put me out of business," Dr. Travis said, walking up to them. "It doesn't get to take vitals check away from me, though." Dr. Travis checked Olivia's vitals, mainly counting the pulse in her wrist, then felt her forehead for a fever. He shrugged at the results, "Any pain?"

Olivia shook her head. "I feel great."

"Well, let me know if you need anything." Dr. Travis said as he left the two of them.

"How did I get here?" Olivia asked Will.

"I wasn't here, but Tiffany said something came and carried you here.'

"Something?"

"Yes, the others saw it. I didn't, they said it looked like a man, a tall man, in a loincloth. They said his face was all wrong though, with big eyes, and his face was pointed.

Had markings painted on his body. Anyway, I guess he carried you here with Tiffany and told them to make you touch the tree. Then he just left."

"A loincloth," Olivia considered.

Will chuckled for a moment, "that's what they said."

"What happened on the road, is everyone ok?

"They're all ok. Everyone made it out. The rabids just kind of retreated for no reason. Spider got pretty banged up, a bunch of bullet holes in him. He's resting inside the wall. We think he's mostly ok, but we can't talk to him."

Olivia nodded, "I'll ask how he is. Rick's dead."

"I heard," Will commented. "Turtle bait. That was a good move by Tiff."

"What about Lewis and Melody?"

"They're ok, Melody was ok, and Lewis touched the tree too. Magic healing tree."

"Tree, a tall man in a loincloth, a lot we don't know yet."

"Do you know where my clothes are, Will? I want to check on the spider."

"Dr. Travis had to cut them off when he was assessing you. Tiffany got you a change of clothes from your room and gave them to him. I'll go find him."

Dr. Travis dropped off the clothes and left. Olivia got her clothes on and stepped out of the tent. Tiffany was standing there, she immediately ran to her, "I thought we lost you." They hugged.

"Is Nina ok?"

"Yes, shaken up. But she's ok. Olivia, thank you for going after her. I was so scared; I just couldn't do anything."

"But you did. You saved your daughter; she would be with Rick and the others now if you hadn't."

"I was so scared of him, I always was. But when I saw you go after him, I realized that's what I should have been doing all along. Protecting Nina from him. I couldn't just sit there and be scared anymore. I couldn't let her be taken away."

"You did it, and now you won't let anyone do that to you, or your daughter again."

"I'll do my best. But it's not over yet. They're still out there, the other rabids. Are they going to come back, Olivia?"

"I don't know, Tiffany. I hope not."

"I know they were after more than just what Rick wanted. You said they wanted to take everyone. I wonder if they still want that…"

Olivia nodded, "I know, honestly I'm worried about that too."

Tiffany nodded at this. "Do you remember that man, or the thing that came?"

"No, Will told me about him."

"It was weird, but I trust it. He wanted to help."

"I'm sure we will see him again soon."

"Olivia," Nina shouted. Running up to Olivia. The hug from the child melted Olivia's heart. Olivia ate some food and then walked around the camp for a while. The people seemed happy and optimistic. Tim had a team of several men working on the well in the center of the town. It was a hole with a three-foot diameter dug several more feet into the ground now. A large stack of sizable rocks was piled next to them, which Olivia could only assume were for the inside of the well and its structure. Lewis was in the hole digging; he had just made some comment that had sent the others standing around into a fit of laughter.

Dr. Travis was talking with Melody, he appeared to be explaining something to her. She thanked him, then walked away. She smiled at Megan, the mother, and the two of them talked for a moment. Olivia couldn't help but think how Melody seemed to have a different posture to herself now. The kids raced past the two of them, Nina in the lead and the two siblings tailing her closely, their laughter was sweet music that caused a smile to form on Olivia's face.

This community that had formed was beautiful, and Olivia wanted it to be kept safe. Wanted the laughter of the kids, the jokes of the men, and the compassion of the women to continue. To not live under the shadow of her brother and his animals. She took a deep breath, and slowly let it out. She knew what she had to do.

"Will," Olivia began, her voice serious. "There's something that I have to do. You're not going to like it."

Will let out a long breath and put down the knife he was using to prep the meat for lunch. "Something tells me you're going to do it even if I don't want you to. Probably easier if you just tell me what it is."

Olivia nodded her head. "I'm going to go to the camp. The rabid camp. I have to confront my brother. I think it's the only way to make this stop. There's a camp of cannibalistic monsters living in our backyard; they will keep coming. I know it. We need to do something."

"We don't have the numbers or the resources to attack the camp, Liv."

"I'm not talking about fighting them. I'm going to go there, confront my brother. Get them to leave us alone."

"How are you going to do that?"

"I'm going to try and convince my brother to come back here and touch the tree."

"You're talking about the cannibal monster brother, right?"

"Tiffany was able to reason with Rick. If I can reason with him. Perhaps we can save him, Will, perhaps we can save all of them."

Will shook his head. "I know you're going to go and do it anyway. I'll go with you if you need."

"I think it's better if I do this alone. If it's just me, I think he will be quicker to reason with me."

Will wiped his hands on a towel, she could tell from his body language that he did not approve. He let out a long sigh, "Ok. I think it's stupid. But, ok."

Olivia walked up to Will and hugged him, the embrace lingered for a moment. "If I don't come back," Olivia said. "I want you to know that I think the Sphere picked the right person to keep us safe. I know that your daughter would be proud of you, Will."

Will looked away and cleared his throat, he pressed his lips together. "Thank you, Liv," his voice a hair away from breaking, he cleared his throat again, regaining his composure. "If you plan on being back before nightfall you should head out now."

"I will, I just need to say goodbye to another friend before I go."

"Liv," Will said.

"Yes," Olivia asked.

"Don't forget to come back to us."

Olivia smiled at him.

"Sounds like a really stupid idea," the spider said, responding to Olivia's plan. "When are we leaving?"

"I'm going alone; besides you're pretty banged up." The spider was near the edge of the camp, it was lying on the ground with its legs tucked under it. It had multiple bullet holes in its body, they were small, considering. Interestingly, they had pieces of cloth covering them. "Looks like they patched you up some."

"I came back with them after the fight, I could hardly move anymore so I sat here. A little while later, they came and put those on me. It helps. I couldn't understand them, and they couldn't hear me. But it was nice of them. Are you sure about going alone?"

'Yes, if anyone comes with me, it may look like a threat. If you come with me, they will definitely react."

The spider chuckled, "Is there something about me people may find threatening?'

Olivia put her hand on the Spider, "I know you're a big teddy bear under there."

The spider was silent for a moment, "Thank you for trusting me, Olivia. I didn't deserve it. I still don't understand why you were so kind to me."

"Everyone deserves kindness."

"I wasn't a good person before all of this, Olivia."

"I was hoping that you would tell me your name before I go, it's weird calling my friend Spider all the time."

"Friend?"

"Yes, you are my friend. I don't know where I would be without you."

The spider, again, stayed silent for a moment, "Brian, my name is Brian. I had the name, Spider, before I turned into one. They called me that because I used to deal, I would do this thing where I would let people try the drugs for free the first time. I did this because I knew that they would like it, and get hooked, then come back for more. I could make customers that way. I would act like I did this because I cared, and just wanted them to have a good time. But really, I just wanted them to keep buying from me. I didn't care how old or young they were. High schoolers, anything. I got lots of kids hooked that way, and people would say that 'Brian caught them in his web.' I didn't mind, I thought it was cool, I even got a spider tattooed on my neck."

"I guess, it all finally caught up to me though. I was going to go to jail, probably prison. I was driving to the college, delivering drugs to this kid that I had gotten hooked. I wasn't paying attention, driving drunk through the college part of town. I hit a girl with my car, she was walking from the park to the campus. She didn't die, but her leg was hurt badly. I heard she had to leave college and have a bunch of surgeries."

Olivia shut her eyes and took a deep breath at hearing this, she could feel tears welling up in her eyes, but she pushed them back.

"I got arrested and was going to go to jail eventually. Waiting for my court date when the Sphere came. When it started singing, it pulled me out of my body, I don't know how else to explain it. The Sphere held me in the air in front of it. I felt like I was standing before a judge, waiting to hear if I would get locked up or not. It told me that I had a choice, my existence could end now - I could fall into oblivion, or I could go back and live, but, if I did go back, it would be in my true form until I was redeemed and worthy of being a man again." Olivia could hear the voice of the spider, of Brian, breaking. Her heart was breaking for him. "I came back, like this. I couldn't talk to anyone, I was alone, and always hungry. So, I hid. I wanted to die; I wished I had chosen oblivion instead. I was trapped in this world, and trapped inside of all the things about myself that were ugly and horrible. I know that now, I used to be so proud to be 'spider,' it was my identity. I thought it made me somebody. But, being tapped inside of it, I hated it. I wanted more than anything to die. Then, you came into the place I was hiding. I don't deserve it, I don't deserve to be your friend, Olivia."

Olivia struggled to hold back the tears, as did Brian by the sound of his voice that she could hear. "Brian," she finally said. "I was that girl that you hit with your car, it was me. And I want you to know that I forgive you, and that you are my friend." Olivia could hear Brian sobbing and the two of them cried together for a short time.

"If you touch the tree, if you go to it, I think it will fix you. You can be Brian again. You can leave 'spider' behind."

Biran seemed to think about this for several moments. "Thank you, Olivia. Thank you, my friend."

2

Olivia's hiking boots sounded out against the broken concrete of the road as she approached the bridge. She had passed the scene of the battle on the road a while ago. The bodies of the rabid were still there, as were the shell casings left behind from the battle. She had quickly walked past that stretch of road. She pondered the house that the crawlers, including her old neighbor Greg, were hiding in. She decided that, if she returned from confronting her brother, she could convince the others to somehow get them to the tree, so it could help them the way it had helped Melody.

She filled her water bottle at the river, the same river where she had been taken by Rick. She took a quick drink and splashed water on her face, contemplating what was to come. She had no weapon; her father's shotgun was most likely still by the pond where she had dropped it when Rick shot her. She had not asked for another weapon before leaving, nor did she try to retrieve hers now. If she survived her brother, she would retrieve it on the way back. She would also take a more thorough rinse in the river when she did, she decided as she felt the cool water relieving the skin on her face.

She crossed the bridge and took the route to their old camp by the river, passing the dilapidated storefront where she first met the spider she now knew as Brian, her friend. She returned to the old camp by the river where she had first met Will, then turned and took the trek through the woods that she and Will had taken when they discovered the rabids' camp. She did this because it was the only route that she knew of to get there. She didn't know the route Rick had taken when he took her from the river.

As she walked through the woods, she reminisced about her brother. About when mom left and he became angry, about how he took care of her while her leg was broken, and how he argued with the nurse in the hospital to get her the things that she needed. No matter what she found at the enemy camp, no matter who this Lord Rage was, she wanted to remember the wonderful moments with her brother. She wasn't ready to let go of Adam, even if Adam was no longer there. She would do everything she could to try and get him to the tree. The tree that redeems. She hoped, hoped in the deepest recess of her soul that he would come to the tree, come and be redeemed.

Yellow eyes and hatred greeted Olivia, none of them attacked her, nor did they even make any attempt to confront or stop her. She assumed this was because they knew Adam wanted her for himself. The horrid mob that had surrounded Olivia before did so again, forming a circle around her and following her as she walked to the large building in the camp where her brother - Lord Rage - ruled. The crowd taunted and screamed, shouted curses and vulgar obscenities at her. She paid them no mind; her mind was set on her goal, and she wouldn't let them derail her. She looked up to the Sphere, the silent sentinel in the sky, and in her mind, asked for it to guide her and give her the strength to do this. She asked for it to soften her brother's heart for what was to come. She prepared herself for the worst, death, or even slavery to her brother. If she had to, she would trade herself for everyone at the camp. In her mind, she held onto the pictures of all the people together, laughing, singing, digging the well, and the children playing. She clung to this like a life raft in a horrible storm, trying to press the crowd that surrounded her out of her mind.

Olivia walked up to the large center structure, the heads of Shiela and Scott still sat on the spikes next to one another. She stood in the mud that she had been kneeling in just a short time ago.

This was it. From the moment she had opened her front door all those days ago, when the Sphere had first changed the world, the moment she stepped out into the world to find her brother, it had all come to this. She had found her brother, and now, she was going to confront him.

"Adam," she shouted. "Adam Jane. It's Olivia, I'm here to talk to you." There was only silence for a moment, then the tarp that covered the doorway of the structure moved to the side, and Adam stepped out.

"Adam," he mused coldly. "That person isn't here."

"I'm not calling you Lord Rage. You're my brother, Adam. Regardless of what you may believe. Or whatever madness has taken over you."

"Suit yourself, Liv. What are you here for?"

"I'm here to negotiate peace." The crowd that was still gathered around laughed and shouted at Olivia in response. Adam raised his pipe into the air and the crowd went quiet.

"Let's listen to your proposal." Adam replied, his voice raised so the crowd could hear.

"You and your people stay on this side of the river, you don't cross or do anything, we won't cross the river and will stay on our side, we won't come over and interfere with anything that you are doing, as long as we both respect the boundaries."

"Hm, and that big spider? Will it respect this boundary?"

"His name is Brian, and yes, he will."

"You named him?" Adam laughed incredulously.

"No," Olivia said firmly. "That is his name."

Adam thought for a second, "And why would I do this, agree to this little peace proposal? Why wouldn't I just order my people to take you captive now, and march my army there and capture and kill who we want?"

"Because it didn't go so well for you last time you tried, your army was pushed back, and you lost your favorite soldier."

Adam let out a cruel laugh, "I see your point, but honestly, Liv, do you really think I wasn't hoping that you would take care of Rick for me?"

Olivia was caught off guard by this. "What do you mean?"

"Rick wanted to replace me and was constantly challenging me. Wanted me dead. Why would I send him on a mission that would let him acquire a family to replace me with?" Olivia thought about this for a moment, it hadn't occurred to her. Adam laughed cruelly again, "What, you thought you defeated my army? It was my plan all along to lead an attack on all of you. I convinced Rick that sneaking in and taking the girl alone was the only way to make it work. I knew you would protect her, the little girl, as well as her mother. You always had a bleeding heart for them. I knew you or they would find a way to stop him, to kill the man vying for my position. My army had orders to make it look real for Rick, and then to return to the camp. Because we are stronger together, the pack must be one," Adam shouted the final comment.

"The pack must be one," the crowd echoed back to him. They hooped and hollered and cried out, waving their weapons, and firing their guns into the air, in a macabre celebration of sorts. They chanted the phrase repeatedly, and Adam raised his arms into the air, as if he were basking in the sound. The sound of his kingdom. He stood like this for several moments, looking at Olivia. He then tapped his pipe hard on the structure behind him, causing a hush to fall on the crowd.

"However, your proposal is interesting. There is much more going on in this world than you are aware of, clearly. Having one less border to worry about would be beneficial to us."

"Eat them, we still could take them for ourselves," a female voice shrilled behind Olivia, she turned and saw that it was the same woman that had been guarding the cages days before, the woman who had helped to kidnap her from the riverside.

"Do we not have plenty from the others we fight? This would be to our benefit, we need not watch all our sides, we can focus on the others." Adam replied, silencing the woman.

"What others, who are you talking about," Olivia asked.

The crowd began murmuring to themselves. "Dear sister, you know so little about this new world. Fear not, I have faith that you will learn in time. You could always stay here, with me, and I will show you all these things."

"Actually, I was going to invite you to come back with me."

The crowd laughed again, as did Adam. "Why would I ever want that?"

"There is a tree there, the tree from our yard. The one that I planted. The Sphere changed it somehow. It's huge. It heals people now. It redeems them. It can do that for you, Adam." Olivia raised her voice and turned to the mob. "It can do that for all of you!" The mob didn't react.

"What makes you think that I would ever want that? To go back to the way things were?" Adam asked. He seemed offended at the notion, and anger seemed to be rising through his calm demeanor.

"Because," Olivia stated, addressing the crowd, too. "You can't be happy like this. Look at yourselves."

"There's nothing wrong with us," Adam shouted back at her, his yellow eyes were taking on an angry intensity. "We are free, you would have us return to the shackles and slavery of weakness that bound us in the old world?"

"No, you wouldn't be slaves, you would be free, truly free. This madness, this evil that you think makes you free isn't freedom. You're in slavery now, you're in slavery to your hate and your anger, to the darkest parts of yourselves. You're not free. Please, Adam, come back with me. Touch the tree, you'll see. You're my brother! I love you! Adam, I have been looking for you since the day all this started. I've been afraid for you. I've cried for you. Please, Adam. Come back with me."

Adam stared at Oliva, a strange stillness had come over him. As if he were deeply contemplating something. For several moments he didn't speak. He stood there, turning a thought over and over in his mind. He then scoffed, and the hardness came over him again. "So," he began, a contemplative shift in his voice. "You never knew. Did you?"

"What are you talking about?"

"He always told me that you didn't know, your dad. I always had my doubts. I knew he was lying to you, so I always figured he was lying to me as well."

"Dad?" Olivia asked. "What did Dad do?"

The cruel smile returned to Adams face. "Your dad, not mine."

"Adam-," Olivia stammered again. "What- "

"Didn't you ever wonder why Mom left so suddenly? How the cow already had a man waiting for her in Arizona? The cow had been having an affair, for years. Then I came. Her little accident. Her little fly in the ointment. She tried to hide it, tried to be smart. Passed me off for his. When your dad found out, she ran off to her other man. She left me behind for her new life."

Olivia's mind spun. She tried to speak, but only mumbles came out as a whirlwind raged in her mind. Unphased, Adam continued. "I found out, I called Mom, confronted her. I wanted to know why she left me behind. You know what the cow did? She hung up on me. Stopped taking my calls. She acted like I didn't exist. I Suppose that was easy for her, she had just started having other kids with him, my real dad. Guess I would have been a problem for her wonderful new life."

"You're not a problem, Adam," Olivia stated, tears beginning to well up in her eyes. It was all she could get out. The only words she could muster.

"I was for your father," Adam replied coldly. Oliva steeled herself for whatever Adam was about to say next. Her whole world was being turned upside down, and she had no idea what could come next. All she could do was brace herself against the next hurtful revelation. "He always loved you more. He was always cold to me. I could never understand why. Until I learned the truth. Guess I can't blame him. I wasn't his. I was just the unwanted leftovers of his ex-wife's affair."

"Dad loved you, Adam." Oliva's voice had grown quiet. She felt as though all her strength had been pulled out of her. All she could do was harden herself. Against whatever was there. She clung to the truth that she knew. She knew she loved her brother. Her half-brother. She clung to that as hard as she could.

"He had to. But I saw the way he looked at me. How the space between us became a million miles and only grew, year after year. But you two. You two became so close afterwards.

"Adam," Olivia started to say, but she was close to breaking now, too close. "Adam."

"You know, when Mom left us, at least she had the decency to move across the country. To truly abandon me. But you, you and him, you stayed down the hall. You were so close, yet you were a million miles away. If your love for me was so great, why, why didn't you come to me? Why weren't you there for me? I was hurting too, but instead of coming to me, or asking how I was, you just buddied up with Dad, you just left me in my room. Did you ever check on me? No, you had all of dad's attention. All his love. You were so happy to take it, but never had any for me. Even when we were together, you got all of it. All his love, all his attention. You both ignored me. You were both right next to me, and none of you ever saw me. At least he had an excuse. But you, you didn't know! It wasn't that you knew and were hiding it! No. You just didn't care."

"Adam," Olivia could feel tears coming, she no longer had the strength to push them back. The female rabid quietly cackled in amusement at Olivia's tears. "I thought you wanted to be left alone."

"I was alone! I was all alone! All I had was you, my only real family, but you were too busy. On your hiking and hunting trips. I came sometimes, and still I was alone. Sitting in a crowded car, completely by myself. You two were so busy taking care of each other, making sure you were both ok, you forgot to be there for me."

The tears were coming down Olivia's face, she could feel herself shaking. "Adam, I'm sorry. I'm sorry for everything. I'm sorry I wasn't there. I'm sorry I didn't know. I didn't know you were suffering. I thought you just wanted to be alone. I thought you were just angry-."

"I was hurting, and alone. You and Dad were both too scared of me to even bother and ask how I was. Because I was mad? Of course, I was mad! Our mother abandoned us. Her! The woman that was supposed to be there for us, to love us. She read books to me as a kid, took care of me when I was sick, she told me that she loved me and would always love me. And then she left me. Left me, left me like I meant nothing! She was supposed to love me, like she promised she would. Of course I was angry! How could I not be angry? But the worst part, the worst part was watching you and Dad love each other.

Neither of you loved me enough to try, to try and reach me. I was hurting and sad, and you didn't even bother to help me because it would be too hard. I wasn't worth fighting for, so you abandoned me. Just like Mom did. You've always loved me, you say? From my perspective, I watched you spend our whole lives avoiding me."

Olivia fell quiet, everything in her was broken hearing this, she was so broken that she felt numb. "I'm sorry, Adam."

"Now, you come here? Now, you ask me to come back with you? To be healed? To go back to the way things were? Never! No, I will never be that weak little boy who was alone again. Too weak and scared to take what he wanted. The day the Sphere came and started singing, I realized what I could be. I could be strong; I could be powerful. My anger, my rage," he said, tapping the pipe hard against the ground. "These things would help me forge a new family, a family that would see me. I started with Rick, and now there are all of us. We are all the outcasts, all filled with the crap and pain from the old world. Now we are together, we are strong, and no one will hurt us. We have the power; we will never be weak again. The pack is strong! The pack must be one!"

The crowd around Olivia chanted the phrase. "The pack is strong! The pack must be one! The pack is strong! The pack must be one! The pack is strong! The pack must be one!" Looking into their faces, Olivia couldn't help but wonder. Did they all feel the same way as Adam? Were they all not monsters, but people who had been hurt, whose spirits, life, and the world that came before had broken? People whose experiences had made them angry, broken, and jaded. Was this crowd of yellow-eyed monsters, in fact, a sea of hurt and trauma that she was gazing into? Not monsters, but hurt people whose pain and angst had manifested into this? Were each of them broken, in their own way?

And wasn't that the way of life? Before the Sphere came, people were controlling, cruel, and rude. People who treated each other poorly, who behaved selfishly. People filled with malice and envy. Was there not pain and trauma that made them that way? Was that what the Sphere brought out in these people? Were they all just people who had let themselves be ruled by their pain? Did the Sphere simply give them what they wanted, and turn their minds over to it?

"Go back to your home, Liv. Go back and let them know that we will stay on this side of the river. You have your family, Liv, and I have mine. Go, now." Without any further comment, Adam, her brother, her half-brother, who she loved, turned and disappeared back behind the tarp. The crowd continued to chant their mantra as Olivia turned and returned the way that she had come, they shouted and cursed at her as they had before. Olivia felt nothing. Her very soul felt shell-shocked from the experience. The foundations of her world felt crumbled, and unsteady.

At a slow, rather mournful pace, Olivia made the hike back to the spot of the old camp next to the river. Her thoughts swam with the realization of what Adam had said.

She didn't want to be, but she was angry at her father. Why hadn't he told her. She wouldn't have stopped loving Adam. Did he not want her to be angry with mom? Was he afraid that she would treat Adam differently? Why? She kept thinking about their childhood. It was true that she and Dad had kept their distance from him. He had been hard to talk to, and often was snippy with them. But still, she should have tried. She could have tried for him. She could have told him she didn't care how snarky and mean he was. She could have fought for him. Her mind was tossed into a dizzy spell.

If he wouldn't let her in, how was she supposed to reach him? It was true that she and Dad were always closer, but that was because they would communicate with each other. Adam didn't let them in, what was she supposed to do? She could see both sides, hers and his. But neither seemed to be the complete truth any longer. His perspective, and hers. There was a divide between the two, and Olivia was drowning in it.

She made it to the river, stripped off her clothing, and went in. She waded out to the center and submerged her whole body under the cold current. She stayed under there for a few moments, then let out a scream. The scream came from deep within herself, and was filled with all the things she could no longer bear. All that she had been feeling. Every inch of the tumult that had formed inside of her. When she was out of air, she came up, took another deep breath, then went back under, and let another cry rip out of her mouth, bubbles containing her anguish exploding from her mouth and hitting the surface of the river. She did this one more time, before returning to the surface, letting as much of her hurt out as she could in that last underwater cry and anguish. She rinsed herself as best as she could in the water, then returned to the back. and dried off with her flannel before putting her clothes back on.

She carried her pants, socks, and hiking boots across the river, then put them on when she was on the tree side of the water. In the distance, she could see the tree, looming over the landscape ahead. She felt a ping of hurt as she looked at it. She had hoped to bring her brother here, to touch the tree and have him healed of his yellow-eyed madness. Her plan for his salvation, for his redemption was impossible now. Olivia felt something in her chest, a truth that was pushing into her. She had felt it before and was feeling it again. Silently, this truth spoke to her: *You can't control him; you can only control yourself. Help those you can. Have faith.* Olivia looked up at the Sphere, this strange thing that had started all of this. She closed her eyes and decided to trust.

As Olivia was walking away from the river and into the long grass field, she got the feeling that something was watching her. She turned to face the riverbank she had just left and came face to face with a very tall human figure. It had the appearance of being a human male, though the face was different. Its face was angular, with a pointed nose and chin, and very high cheekbones, even his hairline was angled in a dramatic widow's peak. Its eyes were also large, and the brightest shade of blue that Olivia had ever seen, standing out in contrast to its olive skin tone. Long black hair fell past its shoulders and had been braided in places. The figure was incredibly tall, perhaps eight or nine feet,. A large loincloth and a chest piece that was made from woven leather were his only items of clothing it wore. He had symbols drawn on his body, long lines with large circles at their ends, on his forehead was a symbol that resembled two circles within one another.

For several seconds, the figure did not move, only stared motionless at Olivia, who in turn stared back. It then tapped its chest twice with one of its long arms, and drew a large circle in the air in front of it, and then pointed to the Sphere above. It held this position for several moments, seemingly waiting for a response from Olivia. To Olivia, it seemed obvious that he was indicating some significance that he had with the Sphere, almost as if his gestures said: me, together, Sphere.

Though this seemed like a clear statement to Olivia, she couldn't understand what it meant in this context. Was he asking if she felt the same way too? Was this a territorial statement? She decided this wasn't a territorial threat, after all, this seemed to be the thing Tiffany had described as having helped carry her back to the tree. So, the statement of allegiance seemed to be the logical choice. Olivia asked herself, do I feel the same? Do I feel that I trust and respect the Sphere? Her conclusion was quick. She felt that she did.

Olivia decided to acknowledge this being the only way she understood how to communicate with him. She repeated the gesture to him, who was still standing on the opposite bank waiting. When she completed it, he bowed his head down. Then, he turned and disappeared swiftly into the forest behind him.

3

She walked back to the camp, grabbing her shotgun that had been left in the long grass next to the pond when she did, though she was careful to not get too close to the pond. She arrived back at the camp, and told Will about what had happened, about the truce they now had with the Rabbids. With her brother. Everyone in the camp rejoiced at this news. And the hope and excitement that went through the camp did indeed warm Olivia's soul. Tiffany appeared and hugged Olivia very tightly, then she scolded her briefly for not telling her what she had planned to do, then thanked her for the results of the plan.

"Liv," Will said. "There is someone that you should meet. Well, you've technically met them before." A man walked up to Olivia, his face seemed nervous, and his posture was cautious. He had a closely buzzed head, with tattoos covering his arms. On the side of his neck, was the tattoo of a spider.

Olivia smiled at him, and the man's brown eyes, of which there were now only two, lit up a little. "Hi, Brian. It's nice to meet you."

Brian, smiled brightly, "Hello, Olivia." They both hugged one another.

"Hey, are you still going to hold your leg up in the air when you talk," Mitch asked Brian.

Everyone, even Brian, let out a bit of laughter at this.

That night, a large meal was prepared, everyone ate and sang along with Lew as he played songs on the guitar. There was laughter, there was joy, but most importantly, there was hope. Hope for the new world that the Sphere and its song had created.

Months passed by and the well was completed, and fresh water was available in the camp. The old homes had been torn down, including Olivia's, and new ones were built. New people, survivors from all around came and joined the town. A garden helped to feed the people, and the community grew its identity as a place of survivors and safety.

4

Silently, it dangled above the world. Much had changed since it came to this blue world, here, alone amongst the stars. It had infused itself into the world, trying to heal much of the hurt. Now, it would seem, a new scenario had come. Old things that had come into new life were now finding their places, in their new forms, in this new world.

Amongst the beings that lived down there, some were aware of the truth of things, some could only see a little, and some could see nothing. It helped to enlighten those who were open to hear and awake to see, and it decided it would continue to do so. It would remain and if called on, it would reveal its truth to others. It was no longer alone; it now had a connection with the beings in this world. And that connection was now the most important thing to it. It would cherish and cultivate this to any who would be open to it.

The darkness had also endured. It was taking a new form now. The darkness of old. It would continue to grow again. Unless it was stopped. It knew it couldn't stop it. Not on its own.

Looking at the past, it could see the presence of the creator, the one who made it. It could see that He would return to His world. Return to it, and to all the beings in this world. It would stay here, waiting for Him to return.

Coming Soon: Book Two

<u>Lacrimosa</u>
A League of Nations